D0239494

THE LOUDEST SOUND AND NOTHING

The Loudest Sound and Nothing

STORIES BY

CLARE WIGFALL

faber and faber

First published in 2007
by Faber and Faber Limited
3 Queen Square London WC1N 3AU

Typeset by Faber and Faber Limited
Printed in England by Mackays of Chatham, plc

Caro at the Pool first appeared in the *Sunday Express*, December 2001.
Free was first published in the online magazine *No Innocent
Bystanders*, January 2005, and in *The Dublin Review*, June 2005. *Hero
I Have Lost* was first published in the Irish magazine *Image*, October
2002. *Night after Night* was originally commissioned by The Watershed
Partnership for broadcast on BBC Radio 4. *The Ocularist's Wife* was
first published in *X-24: Unclassified*, edited by Tash Aw and Nii
Ayikwei Parkes, March 2007. *On Pale Green Walls* was originally pub-
lished as *Her and the Baby* in *Prospect*, December 1997, and later in
Tatler, October 2002. *A Return Ticket to Epsom* was first published in
The Dublin Review, June 2005. *Safe* was first published in *To Hell*, 1,
November 2006. *Slow Billows the Smoke* originally appeared in
Magpie – New Writing, an anthology of work from the UEA Masters
degree, published by CCPA, October 2000. *When the Wasps Drowned*
was first published in the British Council's anthology *New Writers* 10,
March 2001, then in *Voyager*, the British Midland in-flight magazine,
and again in *Turning the Corner: A Collection of Post-Millennium Short
Stories*, Cambridge University Press, July 2007.

Every effort has been made to trace the copyright holder of the poem
'The Story of Bonnie and Clyde' by Bonnie Parker (1934) reprinted in
this volume. The publisher would welcome any information in this
regard.

A CIP record for this book
is available from the British Library

ISBN 978–0–571–19630–2

10 9 8 7 6 5 4 3 2 1

For my family, with love

Contents

The Numbers 1
The Parrot Jungle 19
Caro at the Pool 45
The Ocularist's Wife 51
When the Wasps Drowned 73
Folks Like Us 81
Safe 99
The Party's Just Getting Started 113
Night after Night 125
The Loudest Sound and Nothing 133
A Return Ticket to Epsom 145
My Brain 151
On Pale Green Walls 163
Slow Billows the Smoke 173
Norway 187
Free 207
Hero I Have Lost 213

Acknowledgements 229

THE LOUDEST SOUND AND NOTHING

The Numbers

NUMBERS

ALL THAT I KEN OF NUMBERS I LEARNT AFORE
the age of 10. 1st on an abacus it was taught me, the instrument propped on the lady schoolteacher's desk. After, we progressed to numerals, copying the digits cannily on our slates with pieces of chalk, and rubbing at the answers with our sleeves if we made a miscalculation. The lot of us could fit on 2 benches at 1 time – wee 1s on 1 end, the seniors on the other. That's how wee the school is. Addition, subtraction, division, multiplication; I was always fond of numbers.

When I was 9 I received a prize for recitation of the multiplication tables: a gilt-edged book donated by a religious mission on the mainland. *Spiritual Salvation* the book was called. They kent we were a godless folk, but it didn't stop them trying. Faither placed the prize on the mantelshelf for safe keeping because we'd never had a book in the cottage afore and daren't to dirty the pages of this 1 by handling it, but after some time the soot from the fireplace clouded the paper dustjacket black, and the heat made the cover-boards curl. You could say it was a shame, but the truth is there are worse things have happened in this world.

There were some on the island who wondered what we

might need numbers for. These were the 1s who had never learnt to work with them in their day. They could count on their fingers if they were lucky, and hadn't ever felt lacking in their lives. They didn't approve of filling our heads with a subject so vague-like as numbers. Not that they'd say this afore the lady schoolteacher, mind, because she hailed of good family from the mainland; and besides, the woman was so awfy bonnie. Miss Galbraith was what she called herself, while the rest of us favoured identification through our faithers. Peigi daughter of Finlay is what they call me, Peigi NicFionnlaigh. The women held their tongues in Miss Galbraith's presence and tried to affect that they were gentlewomen, and the men kept quiet altogether, which is a rare thing, I can tell you, and I believe was because they felt themselves abashed, she being that upon which they found themselves hankering when they awoke all feverish from a particular type of night-dream. (I ken this to be true because my brother Iain told it to me when he was 14.)

Thus it continued that the lady schoolteacher would teach us numbers, and we'd learn them until we were 10 and it came time to leave the schoolhouse. And beyond that, apart from the odd occasion when you wanted to count out the eggs to bag up for the mainland, or read the clock perhaps, or work out how many ewes you'd lost in a sudden frost, you could say that numbers weren't of much use to us. Not practically speaking, that is. Which means that in the eyes of many there's little excuse for my fondness. Yet the way I view it, numbers lend a logic to the world. They explain things. Throw light upon problems and make you recognise truth. They can be a comfort.

Take, as example, the issue of marriage. There are 33 of us on the island, myself included. Of these, 6 are kin. Of the remaining 26 (I've subtracted myself), 10 are below the age of 15 and can thus be excluded. 8 remaining are male. 5 of these are wed already. 8 − 5 = 3. 3 unwed males above the age of 15, 1 of whom, it should be noted, is feeble-minded, 1 of whom is unreasonably ugly and kent for his crabbit temper, 1 of whom has been widowed already a good 4 decades, and all 3 of whom are owerly fond of whisky – although that last could be said of almost all the male folk on this island (some of the women folk, too), so perhaps shouldn't be held against them. But you grant where the arithmetic is leading me?

Which is the beauty of numbers. They lay down the facts with such plainness and order you realise it's simply not worth upsetting yourself ower. Even if the solution isn't quite to your liking, in the end it is just a question of arithmetic. Simple arithmetic. Numbers.

And who would be foolish enough to rail against numbers?

BOOTS

When I was 7 and a ¼ a team of men came to our island. They were from a place called Cambridge, they told us, which is in England. We kent about England from the geography instruction the lady schoolteacher had learnt us. We kent our country was divided into 4, and that England was down near the bottom and that they have such things as motorcars there, which are vehicles rather like a dray but which can move of their own accord.

These men wore their face hair clipped into neat shapes and had coloured belts of silk tied about their necks and spoke to 1 another in a language we couldn't understand.

They walked across to the north side of the island and erected a wee canvas tent beside the blackened tarry limb that our men had uncovered some 2 seasons back while cutting peat, and left untouched out of deference to a body taken afore his time.

I have told you we are not a religious folk, and believe not in the existence of gods in the sky above, but there is not 1 child on this island who does not ken of the darksome boggarts who lie beneath us. They bide in the peat bogs, and are looking for any opportunity they can to lay their fingers upon life and pull it to the depths they do inhabit. They are clever, we are told, sleekit with it, and on foggy nights they have been

3

kent to call in thin voices to those they wish to lure unto them. Men, walking home late of an evening, tight after a few drams of whisky, have heard the voices of young lassies calling to them from the fog. Tempting them with that which they desire. It takes a steely heart to walk by.

I once saw a bull that had stumbled into a bog. It was sunk neck-deep already by the time it was found, and was slipping deeper so very slowly it almost looked as if it wasn't going anywhere. It took 8 men to haul the creature out, their ropes looped about his horns.

These men from England did not own the caution of our menfolk. They set about the peat with metal tools and scrapers and eventually were able to lift a body from the clutches of the dank soil once liquidy enough to drown this poor soul. We islanders were allowed to observe their prize. It looked asleep, its spine curved like the line of a ram's horn and the knees pulled up against the chest. The skin was a horrid black-broon with a silver-grey shine to it, and drooped upon the bones beneath like the flesh of a fruit that has turned. The hair was red-broon, but without any shine, like a hank of wool afore it has been spun. Upon its feet remained a pair of leather boots, black-broon like the rest of the body.

I stood afore the trestle table and stared and stared. We had been instructed not to touch. The adults too, as if they were children needed learning. So I don't ken what came ower me, but the truth is there are instances when you are propelled by possibilities you might ken are without reason. I moved my hand swiftly, as if it were a dare made to me by Iain or Mairead. As quickly again my faither slapped my hand away. 'You think you'd like it?' he scolded. 'To be stared at like that? And then prodded by a horrid wee lassie?' And he cuffed my ear sharply as if I deserved the blame for everyone's curiosity.

HERRINGS

Each January sees the beginning of the herring season. Salt herring is what we eat most nights, alongside tatties, and is responsible, some say, for the stomach crampings so many of us suffer from. The drifters from the mainland ports return laden with catches of the fish that must be gutted and packed in barrels of salt for export.

If the north wind is not too squally, a boat is sent ower and us girls, or those that can be spared, go athwart to help with the gutting.

Ower a decade now I have been aiding at the gutting, and yet I still have not found my sea legs. I am afeared of the water, and confess the journey is a torment for me, with the boat tipping us this way and that, and myself praying my stomach shan't pitch my breakfast porridge ower the edge.

Last year was no exception. I left the cottage afore sunrise, and walked 4 miles in lantern-light to reach the beachfront. I couldn't help but count the steps down to the shore, and told myself that if the final tally was even, the journey athwart the water would not drown us. The final step was odd. But then I considered the return journey I would have to make that night, and agreed with myself that I could factor this into the sum, allowing me to multiply the number by 2. After that I felt much more at ease.

3 other girls were waiting already, their faces pinched against the cauld and drizzle, their shawls wrapped tightly around them. The bonnie sisters Anna and Caìtriona NicPhàdraig were there. And young Màiri, daughter of Alasdair the fiddler, who was joining us for her 1st gutting. Maureen NicAindreas, Domhnall MacAindreas's feeble-minded sister, was absent. We all agreed this was for the best, considering the incident at the previous year's gutting. It had been discomfiting for all involved. Besides, Maureen had been laid poorly for some time and we none of us had seen too much of her for a while.

We shared some pleasantries, and in the gloaming of the early dawn saw the rowboat coming towards us athwart the waves.

*

You will imagine my surprise when I found I recognised the fellow at the tiller. Willeam MacGhobain, who studied in the schoolhouse with me. I remembered him a bone-pale timid laddie, who caught the croup when he was 13 and was sent ower to his aunt on the mainland where he could be nursed in the hospital. A few of the other schoolchildren used to take a rise out of me on occasions, once or twice driving me into quite a temper, saying that Willeam held something of a fancy for me. But after leaving us, he never returned to the island, and I had not spared him too much thought in the years that had past.

With the oars in his gloved hands, he was still pale as I remembered him, but harsh winds and cauld weather had thickened his skin. He had a long sheepish face now, with yellow hair sticking which-way from his crown. Even his eyebrows and lashes were yellow. He lifted a hand to help each 1 of us into the boat, and as he took my own and looked up at me I saw recollection flash athwart his face. To my great shame, he blushed like a lassie.

I dipped my head as I took my seat and let go his hand quickly, but out of the corner of my eye I could see the red flushing at his cheekbones and creeping along the curlicues of his ears. 'Why,' I thought to myself, 'he is just as foolish as ever he was.'

'Willeam MacGhobain?' I said to him, hoping the other girls had paid no heed to his colouring. 'It is a full 14 years since we saw each other last, is it not?' Which meant that I had *not* kent him for 1 full year longer than I had kent him, so really I did not ken him very well at all.

The others in the boat were a good deal younger than us, and thus had never afore seen Willeam in their lives, but we 2 spoke as he pulled us athwart the grey water.

'You are not married?' he asked, for married women do not so normally go athwart to the gutting.

I replied that I was quite content as I was, and very busy with it. My faither would surely not get by without me now our mother was gone. I explained that Iain had taken ower the croft, and had a cottage nearby with his wife and their 3 young 1s.

'And you had a sister,' he said.

'We lost Mairead,' I told him, but did not feel able to say more on that matter. Besides, the wind was up, and the tipping of the boat was rather beginning to affect me. I took a deep breath to steady my wits, and as solace reminded myself that the number of steps had come out even. Then I counted 8 a few times in my head, for good measure. Anna and Caìtriona were singing – a hearty sea ballad – and I wondered how they could manage it. 'You must have a wife and family, no doubt,' I ventured, so he wouldn't think me snubbing him, 'ower on the mainland?'

Now it was his turn to look away, and for the wind I barely heard him tell me that his wife had passed.

He came at the end of the day and took us home. 'You will come again tomorrow, Peigi NicFionnlaigh?'

'I daresay,' I told him. 'And you will row the boat, Willeam MacGhobain?'

'I daresay,' he replied with a smile.

I tried not to think about that smile on my walk home. The fog had crawled in, and the path was hard to see, even in the light of my lantern. It is dangerous to let your concentration slip on such a night. But I found my mind turning ower the things that he had told me, and imagining his life on the mainland, living in that tall brick house with his 2 wee motherless bairns and his maiden aunt who was suffering so now from arthritis.

So occupied was my mind, I almost didn't hear the voice in the fog.

At 1st I thought it a wee beastie. A lamb that had got lost, perhaps, and was greiting for its mammy. But it wasn't the lambing season. I held up my lantern in the rainy mist and listened. I ventured the sound could be far off perhaps, carried on the fingers of the wind. There was naught to be seen beyond the yellow halo the fog made about my lantern. Again came the sound. A thin, eerie wail. A chill shivered through my bones and my breath quite stopped.

I listened, and now I could hear nothing beside the wind howling athwart the treeless land. 'You're letting your foolish imagination carry you away, Peigi daughter of Finlay,' I told myself sharply, and turning back to the path took a few hurried steps, wanting to be home and in the warm, cooking up the herrings in my bag for Faither. But then it came again. Closer this time it seemed, or louder at least. A sound quite aching with loneliness.

My feet halted. 'You silly creature, ignore it,' I said out loud. 'It is nothing but the call of the darksome boggarts trying to trick you. Walk on. Walk on, you foolish girl!' But my heart would not allow it. The thin cry I heard in the darkness touched a deep and trembly chord inside me, and against all sense and reason I could nay ignore it.

Each step I took from the path was made cannily, 1 toe feeling ahead to confirm solid ground, and betwixt each step I paused to listen for the sound. Sometimes, it seemed louder, at others it would hush completely. 'Helloo?' I called into the night. 'Be anyone there?' But the wind seemed to carry my words instantly up and away into the dark sky.

I had taken 8 paces 3 times ower into a fog that closed behind me with each step I took, and kent that the further I went, the harder it would be to find my way back. I confess I was just about to gather my senses and turn around again when I saw in the lantern light a dim pale shape on the ground before me. Silly thing that I am, it made me leap. I thought it perhaps a wraith, crouching before it jumped at me, but the shape did not move. I daresay I have never felt so afeared in my life. But I had come this far, and kent I could nay turn back. I knelt carefully, set my lantern upon the gorse, and inched my hand forwards through the dense fog. What my cauld fingers touched was a rough woollen blanket, the oldest blanket you could imagine. All torn and dirtied and studded

8

with burrs as if it had lined a cowshed. I pulled back 1 corner and that which I found made me gasp.

This was no spectre beneath my fingertips. No darksome boggart. No wraith. This was flesh and blood.

Disturbed by the icy draft, the wee infant began again at its greiting.

POTATOES

When my grandmother was a wee lassie, a blight turned the potatoes soft. She could recall helping her parents to pull them from the earth. Tattie after tattie, each 1 shrivelly and thread-ed with rot. They sorted through them to see if any could be salvaged, then collected the rest into a pile in 1 corner of the croft and left them there. Her parents talked of quitting the island, of taking a boat as others were doing far athwart the seas to a land called Canadia. But our family have lived on this island for generations, and my grandmother's elders were not certain they could conceive of a life beyond it.

She was never schooled, my grandmother. The schoolhouse was closed for cause of the blight. It was not a time for educa-tion, and besides, the children of the island were too weak to walk all that way each day. Thus she never learnt about arith-metic, she never learnt how to read a page from a book, she never learnt geography, she never even learnt to write her name. But my grandmother could sing. Even in later years her voice was clear and tempered like the movement of water through a burn. 'Ach, I filled my empty stomach with song,' she told me, explaining how she survived when so many oth-ers did not.

There were lullabies she used to sing to me, songs that had been sung to her by her own mother, and that she had sung to my mother afore me. I remember lying beneath the blankets in the same bed I sleep in now but at that time shared with Iain and Mairead. I can recall with great clarity the crackle of the fire and the sound of my grandmother's voice as I fought to keep my eyes from drooping.

I sang those same lullabies to the baby, and they seemed to soothe her. 'Hee balou,' I hushed. 'Hee balou.' So wee was she. So very fragile I feared she might break. The dome of her head pressed slightly, it was not firm like my own, and the broon hair was like the softest down you can imagine.

At 1st Faither wanted naught to do with her. He told me to take her back out again and leave her where I'd found her, but I told him straight I would do nothing of the sort, and in the end he had to let it be for he could see I was full determined, and he is an old man now, and no longer as strong as he once was. I told him to banish his ridiculous fancies from his head and fill the biggest cooking pot we had with water and warm it on the fire.

She was wee enough to fit right in the pot, and I joked that she could make a bonnie stew. Faither laughed at that. He hadn't had his herrings yet and I daresay he was awfy hungry. All the while, as he helped to scoop the water ower her, I was taking care to hold her safely, and support her head. I was not used to holding such a wee infant, especially when slippery with water and soap. I counted each finger and toe, and all was perfect. 'She is not long of this world,' Faither told me. 'Only a day or so, I would venture.'

As we were drying her afore the fire, she started again to whimper and we agreed she must be hungry, so while I wrapped her in a pillowslip and then the softest blanket I could find, Faither went out and fetched a cup of milk from the cow. I used my little finger and a silver teaspoon to drip it in her mouth and it seemed to calm her until eventually she fell to sleep in my arms.

'You will have to cook the herrings,' I told Faither. 'For I don't think I can move.'

Superstitions

For sure all folk ken that 2 crows flying ower a house foretells a wedding, or that a grave dug on a Sunday will lead to another being dug for the body's kin afore the week is out, or that a slip of rowan tied with a red thread and kept on 1's person on the eve afore May Day will be a charm against ill luck and avert evil from 1's flocks and herds. We grow up with these superstitions. We learn them afore we even ken they are being taught. We all put on our right shoes 1st of a morning without ever asking ourselves why.

It is bad luck to let the moon shine on an infant's face, or to have them sleep in a new cradle. Their clothes should be passed through a fire, and a dobbet of butter should be dropped in their mouth and swallowed if they are to be protected from malignant spirits.

I did all that which I could for her.

But still my brother Iain warned, 'Peigi, folk will not take well to that bairn. Not when you found her in the mist like you did, with no indication of where she might hail from, and that blush you won't acknowledge upon her face. There is some darksome magick surrounding her and she'll bring bad luck to the island, that's what they will say.'

I turned from him and walked back alone to the cottage, holding the baby close against my chest.

They came to look her ower. I kent they would. And of course I could not turn them away from the door, that would not be proper. We went flat through our supply of tea-leaves, and my arm was quite aching from the pouring of whisky. I cooked butter-saps in the pan, always a dainty at a new birth, until we were out of oatmeal.

Out of politeness they kept their tongues quiet, but I saw the looks between them, and when I quit the room to check on her, lying in the cradle begged from Iain and his wife, the walls weren't thick enough to block out the speculatings Iain had predicted. To drown their words I counted 8 ower and again. I did look hard at her bonnie wee face, but I could see no darksome magick.

Domhnall MacAindreas even came to our door, and he has certainly never shown interest in a bairn afore. There is little amity shared between the 2 of us, and never has been. A rough, ugly man, with a temper to match. His horrid eyes have a way of lingering on your flesh.

'Folk are saying you've found a bairn out in the fog, Peigi NicFionnlaigh, with the markings of the Deil upon its gruntle, isn't that so? I thought I'd better come and have a wee look.'

'Are you sure it's not our whisky bottle you are wanting a wee look at, Domhnall MacAindreas?'

'Ach, but I'll be wanting a look at that too, for sure I will. But 1st this bairn.' And he stepped inside without even wiping his boots.

I didn't like his manner, but I felt obliged to show him through to the bedroom. As he pulled back the coverlet from her chin with his hairy fat fingers, a crabbit look came upon his face. I had to halt myself from spitting at my handkerchief to rush and wipe at her cheek where he had touched.

'Oh, but Peigi NicFionnlaigh,' he said unpleasantly, 'no good will come of this 1. No good at all.'

I didn't see this to be a comment fit for reply.

I cleared 9 plates and 12 glasses and 2 spent whisky bottles at the end of the night, and found just 1 glass unemptied. The wee 1 Mother used to favour, with a lick of blue paint around its rim. It was the glass that Domhnall MacAindreas had been sipping from. That man has nay been kent to leave even a single drop at the bottom of his whisky glass, so I kent he'd done so out of spite. For all folk ken that it is dangerous to the health of a newborn bairn not to finish your glass.

I had missed 1 full week of the gutting. And as I walked again athwart the hills I realised I had not thought once about Willeam MacGhobain. In fact, it seemed a lifetime now since that morning when I'd 1st climbed into his boat and said helloo. I wondered if he had noted my absence.

As I drew closer to the beachfront, I began to grow apprehensive, and had to count 8 for a while. The others surely would have spoken to him already. I had to stop myself from running the last stretch because I wanted to grab him and shout, 'No, none of it's true. She's nay bad luck, that's foolish talk. There's naught unnatural or darksome about her. She's beautiful. Beautiful. You'd ken it too if you could see her!'

But to my shock, as I took his hand and climbed into the boat, I didn't see that look of discomfit that I expected. Instead he smiled, that halting smile of his, and asked me what I'd called her.

'Sine,' he repeated after me, as if he wanted to taste the sound of the word in his mouth. It is our word for gift.

'Sine,' I replied.

MILK

He came on a gustery afternoon.

I was alone with her, Faither having gone up on the croft to help Iain with a sickly ewe. The sky was greying up outside, and I'd been forced to light the lamp. I had a batch of wool for carding, but 1st wanted to set a pan of milk on the fire to warm because I could tell she'd be getting hungry. You would not believe how she had grown. How healthy the wee creature was looking.

The shock of him banging at the door like that caused me to spill the milk all ower the hearthstones. Like a madman he was banging, and a moment later he came storming through the door, letting in the wind and the cauld with him. 'Where be the bastard?' he roared. 'Where is it hiding?'

I have never seen a man so filled with fury. His eyes were blazing with it, and it seemed to charge the air about him. He burst into our wee living room afore I could say a word. Cursing, he knocked against the side table, and in his anger hurled it athwart the room so it broke in 2. His hair was all uncombed, and he was reeking of drink, his breath dank with it. Unwashed he was too. I could smell the sweat and grease of him, like the wool afore it has been soaked. He was like a man possessed, not seeing of me at all, just focused on his purpose.

His voice was raging and his words coarser than any I'd ever heard spoken by any man.

They asked me later why I did nothing, but what they don't understand is that it all happened so fast.

He saw the basket beside the fire and grabbed for her, his hairy fingers snatching her from the cushions and shaking the poor thing as if she were little more than a sack of potatoes.

I did cry out. That I did. But his arm smacked me sharply around the head so I fell hard against the wall, and by the time I had arisen he was already out the door again.

I ran straight after them, hollering at him to let me have her back, but he is a big man, Domhnall MacAindreas, and more than once he sent me reeling. I was like the irritation of a fly to him, easily swatted away.

I could not catch him, even stumbling as he was for all the drink in him. And I tell you how I did try. I grabbed at his shirtsleeves, and caught a lock of his hair, and clung on 1 leg even, afore he kicked me away. I did try to stop him, harder than anything afore in my life.

But then it happened.

When I look again upon it now, in my dreams, in the recollections they forced from me, I see it all occur so slowly. It can nay have been that way, but certainly it was time enough for all colour to drain from my face. He appeared just to wobble backwards a moment on the dry gorse, his arm lifting as he did, and then he let her go and hurled her in a steep arc through the air. Where she fell, the lace coverlet she'd been wrapped in trailed milken athwart the black surface of the peat bog.

'Bastard,' he cried, stumbling, his legs criss-crossing and threatening to topple him. 'Bastard, be gone with ye,' he cursed.

I lost my senses, I'll confess it now. When they pulled me from the bog, my skirts and hands and hair heavy with the thick black sludge, Iain had to slap me about the cheek afore I was able to collect myself again and see the matter straight. There is no use greiting ower spilt milk, was what my mother used to say.

PORRIDGE

I went again this year to the gutting, and again Willeam MacGhobain was at the tiller.

'Greetings to you, Peigi NicFionnlaigh,' he said to me, with a short smile of sadness.

'Greetings, Willeam MacGhobain,' I replied.

The sickness started almost as soon as we pulled away from the shore, and I closed my eyes, feeling sure that this time my breakfast porridge would not have the strength to stay fast.

We did not speak either of us on the journey ower, and I believe it was because he did not ken what words to say to me. But on our return he touched my knee with his fingers as the oar stroked past, and said, 'Why do you count like that, Peigi NicFionnlaigh?'

'Pardon?' I replied, for it took me a moment to work his meaning.

'No,' he said with a shake of his head, 'no matter.' He gave me a smile. 'I heard you were ower on the mainland a few months back.'

'That's correct,' I replied plainly. 'And I don't think I'd be wanting to return. All those folk and filth. I can nay ken how you suffer it.' It had been the 1st time I'd ever ventured beyond the herring yard.

He tipped his head, and I saw the cauldness of my words had hurt him. He always was a soft lad. 'Well, at least it looks as though the trial will reach its proper conclusion,' he said thinly.

'It looks that way.'

He pulled a few more strokes, his mouth tight, his eyes not looking in my direction. I felt suddenly sorry for how I'd treated him, when he was showing only kindness. But I didn't ken how to right it.

'To think that he'd been doing such wicked things with his poor simple sister,' said I. I had to swallow hard, and for sure it must have been the tipping of the boat.

The numbers wouldn't stay straight, they kept jumbling as I tried to order them.

Out of the corner of my eye, I glanced his way again and saw that he was watching me sadly, while his fine strong hands pulled the oars through the dark water.

I felt the lurching of my stomach, and thought how ugly I must look, green with the desire to vomit. My hands reeked of fish guts and salt and harsh carbolic soap. For a moment I thought how easy it might be to simply tip back ower the edge of the boat and sink beneath the grey waves.

But of course now, that would have been against reason.

The Parrot Jungle

CHICKA-CHICKA-CHICKA-CHICKA SING THE numbers on the counter as they rotate in the late-afternoon sun. A man sits in the front seat, listening to the sound. His hands rest loosely at the wheel, and through the clammy fabric of his pant legs his thighs cling to the seat leather. His name is Johannes. He listens to the sound and lets his eyes close, feeling how exhausted his body is, feeling its weight in the dense air. After some moments he turns his eyes to the rear-view mirror, in which he can see the pump attendant standing with the sun on his brow as he waits for the tank to fill.

The attendant's hair is combed back from his forehead and slick. He is gazing at nothing, but his ear is attuned to listen for the slowing in the numbers, and he knows to look up exactly as the counter closes with a weary unfinished *chi–*. He shakes the hose and hangs it back at the pump.

'Guess she's pretty gas hungry, huh?' he says, leaning down to the passenger window. His vowels are all drawn out and looped together, as if the words have melted in the heat. In mute acknowledgment of Johannes's nod, he pulls back again from the window so he can survey the car. 'Don't offen see these old gals no more, do ya?'

Johannes can't see his face any more, only the man's torso framed in the open window; across the breast pocket of his overalls, an embroidered patch reads *Larry*. As he counts out and hands across the money, Johannes asks about somewhere to stay, speaking with an accent that the attendant registers, but couldn't identify if asked. European-sounding, the words shaping themselves neatly near the front of his mouth. Not an unfriendly voice, but one which seems to indicate a certain reserve in the speaker.

'Inter-State Dog Show,' says the attendant with a shrug.

Johannes nods. He'd been told the same in the motel up the road.

He stares forward through the windscreen, at the doorway to the station's tiny convenience store. There are advertisements for Coca-Cola and Dorito chips on the window. Beside a rack of *Arizona Herald* newspapers, in the shade of the awning, is a wooden chair for the pump attendant to rest while he's awaiting custom.

The attendant's forearm is still resting on the window ledge, hanging half into the car, with Johannes's bills crumpled in his oil-stained hand. He is looking at Johannes now, soberly, as if evaluating him, his eyes taking in the blond beard, the hair in need of a trim, the well-cut button-down shirt unfastened at the collar, the excessive tan of his left arm. He sees a tired man who's driven many miles along straight roads through hot country. 'You could try my sister-in-law, if'n you want,' says the attendant. 'She takes in payin' guests sometimes. Name's Lisa. Lives up on Fairbank.' He pulls a slip of paper and a pen from his pocket and rests it on the hood beside the crumpled banknotes. *Lisa Wales*, he writes in loopy grade-school cursive, *Fairbank 1009*.

Johannes pulls up at a stop light before turning onto Fairbank and watches a middle-aged woman wearing an orange plastic sun-visor cross in front of the car. She is walking a squall of small Maltese dogs. Johannes counts at least six of them

20

undulating about her feet, their short legs concealed beneath long fur. They remind him of Hokusai clouds, or it could be waves, maybe even snow. For a second or two he can't see them as dogs any more, only the crash and curl of snow-white surf in a Japanese print.

The light changes and he makes a left. He is driving on a wide unhurried suburban street, the houses set slightly back off the road. Cacti and pink-flowered shrubs grow in the gravelled front yards. Flags hang outside many of the buildings. He counts the numbers on the fence-posts and mailboxes and crosses four blocks before he comes to 1009.

Parking before a low, putty-coloured house, Johannes climbs from the car. There is a small eucalyptus tree in the front yard. From its branches hang four or five faded windspirals of coloured parachute silk, turning almost imperceptibly in the air. Johannes looks at these as he stretches his shoulders and arms, then closes the car door and walks up the front path.

Across the main entrance to the house is a screen door. Lengths of string are tacked to the top of its wooden frame and suspended on each is a prism of coloured glass that captures the light – six or seven of them in total, each hanging at different heights across the screen. Beyond that, the doorway is open. He looks through the screen into a large living-dining area that stretches right through to the back of the house. The room is carpeted in rust-orange and has two low sofas. There's a circular dining table with four chairs ranged around it, and a bookcase against the wall. The furnishings are outmoded by at least two decades, their edges bleached and haloed slightly by the sunlight flooding through the far windows. It all gives him the odd feeling of staring in at a dated Polaroid photograph.

Beside the doorframe is tacked a lilac-coloured business card. In an ornate font it reads *Liza Wales Cert. Prof. National Council of Geocosmic Research – Answers for the heart . . . from the heart – tel: 480–481–9462 – email: earthmom68@mindspring.com*. Someone has surrounded the writing with tiny stars and hearts drawn in silver marker.

'Hello?' Johannes calls uncertainly, leaning slightly towards the metal mesh of the screen.

He waits a moment and is just about to call out again when a woman's voice strings onto the air, the sound reaching distant from somewhere beyond, 'Gimme a second.' Johannes takes a step back again and looks away along the house front. The air is dry with the heat. A car drives past on the road behind him, and from within the house he hears water splashing and the faint clinking of crockery. A silver-grey cat appears around the corner of the building and steals along the façade, its gaze stalking Johannes suspiciously. It leaps up to a narrow windowsill and sits, unblinking, its eyes like glass marbles flecked dark at the core.

'Hello?'

Johannes turns back to see a woman stepping towards him on the other side of the screen, drying her hands on her skirt as she approaches and peering to make out his figure in the doorframe. She pulls open the screen and the glass prisms swing forward in the air before smacking back against the mesh. 'Hi,' she says, smiling at Johannes. Across her brow a flicker of a frown passes – more perturbed than suspicious – but her smile doesn't falter, 'You here for a reading?'

She speaks with the same rolled vowels as her brother-in-law. A small, slim woman with tan skin and darker freckles splashed across her bare shoulders and cheeks, she looks to be in her mid thirties, and wears a loose mauve cotton vest top, faded from overwashing, and an ankle-length Indian skirt of a fabric fine enough for the light to shine through it at the hem. Her freckled collarbone is pronounced and her eyes are green like her cat's, the eyelids papery. Her hair hangs loose to her shoulder blades. It is wavy, light brown in colour, and looks as if she rarely bothers it with a comb. She has a narrow nose, the bridge pinched, and from her ear lobes hang dangling earrings that swing alongside her neck. Her face is bare of make-up. It has an appealing almost-naked quality that suits the open warmth of her smile.

Johannes is confused by her question. 'I'm looking for a place to stay. Your brother-in-law . . . at the garage –'

'Oh, *Larry*,' she says and laughs. Her fingers are ringed with silver, her wrist looped with a collection of bangles which make a zither of sound as she moves her hand forward. 'I'm Liza.' She pronounces it *Lye*-za, the first syllable stretching long and flat.

'Johannes.' Her hand feels dry as he shakes it, the silver of her rings more solid than her finger bones.

'Well, the room's spare. Those dog people booked up all the hotels?'

He nods.

She shakes her head sympathetically, and lifts a hand to rest it against the doorframe. For a moment she studies Johannes with her pale eyes. 'Capricorn?'

Smiling, she watches him, then laughs again at his confusion, her head bending forward so that for a second her face is curtained by her hair.

'Your *sign*? I'm right, aren't I?'

Her eyes are expectant as they await his answer. 'Yes,' Johannes nods, and smiles back in return, but with the slim awkwardness of one confronted unexpectedly by a faith he doesn't share, as if she had just taken his hand and asked, 'Jesus?'

Soon after Liza showed him to the room, she heard the shudder as the guest shower started working, and the juddering of the water pipes filling. 'Shoot,' she said out loud to herself, 'I should have gotten that fixed.' After that it went quiet. She was working on an astrological chart for Mrs Rosacio in the pharmacy but couldn't focus her thoughts, so after a while she got up to pour herself a glass of milk and picked up the phone.

'Hiya, Doug. How you doing?'

'Why you whispering?'

'I'm not whispering,' she said, raising her voice slightly and turning to the wall. 'There's a man here. I don't wanna waken him.'

'What kind of a man?'

'Larry sent him over. He came into the gas station.'

'And he just sent him to you? He know him?'

'Nu-uh. He just came in. He's from Europe, university professor, teaches at a school in California.'

'You want me to come over? Think I should?'

'Quit it, Doug. Can I talk to Harley?'

'Don't know if I like this, Larry sending strange guys over to you.'

'*Doug.*'

'He could be a pervert.'

'He's not a pervert. Gimme Harley.'

'How do you know?'

'I just do, okay? I wanna talk to Harley, will you give him to me?'

'Lisa.'

'You gonna make me call my son on his cell?'

'Okay, okay. Well look, hey, you call me if you need anything, uh-huh?'

'Uh-huh.'

'Hang on. He's watching TV.'

Opening a bottle of organic red wine she'd had in the fridge since the May County Fair, Liza sits on the porch, closes her eyes to feel the warmth of the golden evening light on her eyelids, and thinks again about the man in her guest bedroom. It was strange how different it felt having another person in the house, even when you couldn't see them, even when they were quiet behind a closed door. It was like the energy in the house was all electric. Like static when you walked across a carpet in socks.

She cracks a pistachio shell, and the sound is loud against the night. It makes her laugh a little, drunkenly, for no reason. A laugh loose like a ribbon falling slack from one's hand. Johannes can't see her face but her legs are lit by the yellow electric light thrown through the kitchen window. They are bare, unshaven, stretched up upon a garden chair.

'Is it always this hot?' he asks eventually.

'Uh-huh,' and again that loose-edged laugh. He feels distanced by her drunkenness. It cocoons her. Like a quilt about her shoulders. She reaches for the bottle and pours more wine in her glass, then sits back again and cracks another pistachio, dropping the empty shell against the ground.

In the shadows around them, cicadas crouch – perched on branches and in the dry grass. Their eyes small like blank beads. He listens to the noise they make, feels the rhythm of it, and finds himself surprised he had not been hearing it before. So loud it seems, now that he is listening to it.

'Always hot,' she says, and without noticing he forgets again to listen to the cicadas. 'You been up to Four Corners?'

He nods.

'Hopscotch across the four states?'

'I stayed in the car.'

'*No*. You stayed in the car?'

'A class of school children were on the monument.'

'School kids? You let a bunch of school kids stop you? Jeez! When else you gonna get a chance to stand in four states in the same hour? Oh, man.' She gives an amused laugh. 'Me, I always wanna try everything. Drives Harley just crazy. He's like his dad – he's not like me. Really mature for his age. Like sometimes I can't believe I got a kid who's so . . . And he's only sixteen. I tell you, he's just like his dad.'

Her voice as she speaks is soft at the edges, low, punctuated by her laughter. It has the quality of pebbles displaced under water.

'You've been apart long, you and his father?'

'Me and Harley's dad? Like split up? Oh,' she laughs, 'oh, yeah. Like Harley was only four when we broke up. It was a *long* time ago.'

'Never remarried?'

'Remarried? No, no, no, no.' Still that laughter slipping between the words. 'No way, not me. Once was enough. I mean, I've had opportunities, but . . . I don't know. Anyway, you get used to things, don't you?' She swirls the wine at the bottom of her glass, then glances down suddenly as she feels something brush against her leg. 'Hey, baby.' It's the grey cat that had been watching Johannes earlier. 'Come on up here,' she says. 'Come to Mommy.' The cat turns up to face her, its eyes flashing flat in the kitchen light like coins at the bottom of a well, then leaps up to her lap and circles before it settles, its claws catching in the fine muslin of her skirt. She strokes the sleek length of its back. 'Want me to read your cards?' she says, not looking up from the cat.

'You don't need to do that.'

'No trouble. Come on, let's do it. I'll get my deck.'

'No, no,' he says again, with something like urgency, and puts out a hand to stop her.

She's watching him, half smiling, her hand paused upon the cat's back. 'You think it's all hooey-fooey bullshit, don't you?' she says after a moment, with amusement in her voice, then laughs out loud to see Johannes's face flush with protest. 'Oh, come on! Those questions earlier? You, sir, with your college degree, you think it's all bullshit, don't you? Admit it. Come on.'

'No.'

'No? Well, I'll tell you something, Mr University Professor,' she points her finger at him, smiling widely, 'I got a woman comes to me each week all the way from Flagstaff and her husband used to be the *dean* at ASU. Every week she comes.'

Johannes is laughing with her now; to dispute would be futile.

'Wife of the dean, huh? So, there you go.' She sighs back into her seat and strokes again at the cat's back. 'No, seriously, hey? It's not for everyone, I know that.'

'Look –'

'Tsh,' she says, to quieten him. 'There's just one thing I don't get, huh? I mean, if you think it's all . . . Well, you know. Then how come it scares you so much?'

'I didn't say that.'

'Didn't have to,' she says in a still voice. 'Hey now, let's forget it, huh? You know what, I'm probably way too drunk to read right now anyhow.' Her laugh comes, easy again. She shakes her hair from her shoulders. 'You want more iced water, hon? Your glass is empty.'

Sitting alone, he listens as she turns on the tap at the kitchen sink, leaving it on to run cool while she goes for the ice, then hears the slam of the freezer door and a bang as she slaps the ice tray against the counter top to loosen the cubes.

He's barely held a single conversation lasting more than five minutes over the past two months. So how strange it is that he should be here now, in a backyard in Arizona, well past midnight, with a woman who reads fortunes for a living.

'I don't normally drink, you know,' she says as she fills his glass, the ice cubes tumbling out of the pitcher.

'You've told me.'

'I have? Shit.' She laughs. 'Anyhow, it's your fault. Only opened the bottle 'cause you were here. Didn't know you weren't gonna share it, that's all.'

She glances towards his glass. 'Don't like talking about yourself much, do you? I like that in a person. Always liked that. Harley's the same. So's his dad.' She cracks another pistachio and lifts it to her mouth. 'So, the university, they don't mind you've just taken off? Don't they expect you to turn up every day?'

He focuses on the wooden edge of the tabletop to avoid her gaze. 'They've given me a sort of sabbatical,' he says after a moment. 'A sort of leave of absence.'

'Is that normal?'

'I needed some time off.'

She considers this. 'Cool.'

He nods.

'So you been to Florida? *No*? You haven't been to *Florida*?' She pronounces the first syllable as if it rhymes with the chlor of chlorine – Flore-i-da. Flore-i-da. '*Oh, my God*, you should go to Florida. Drove Harley there when he was eight. Just him and me, all the way to Florida. God, I *love* that state. They've got there the Parrot Jungle, Monkey Jungle . . . what's the other one? Lion Park Safari? You haven't seen any of those?' He shakes his head and she exhales. 'Man, you are missing out. I'd love to live in Florida, I swear.'

'You could move.'

'Move to Florida? Oh,' she leans back and gives a long sigh. 'Oh, I don't know. I'd sure love to, but his dad's here, and I wouldn't want to take him away from his dad. And you know, I'd have to find new clients and everything, and . . . Maybe I'll do it one day, when he's older. Maybe I'll retire to the Keys, how about that?' He likes how easily her laugh comes. 'I'd like to go soon though. That's the one thing I'd really like to do. Take him while he's still young. See the Parrot Jungle again.'

'What's stopping you?'

'"What's stopping me?" he asks! Well, for one, I haven't even got a car right at the minute. Don't have the money for a new one neither, not even if I bought it on leasing. Used to have a Subaru. A gold Subaru. Used to let Harley drive it and one night last May – no, April it was – he was coming home from some party and wrecked it. He'd been drinking. Hey,' she says, as if suddenly struck by a new thought, 'didn't I tell you earlier that he was real mature?'

'Was he okay?'

'Oh, sure, he was fine. Completely okay. One kid in the back seat had to wear one of those – what do you call them? – those neck braces? For like two months or something. But the rest of them were fine. Just the car was wrecked.'

'Were you angry?'

'Angry? No. He was okay and he learnt something from it. That's all that matters. They took away his license, but he was okay and that's all I was gonna care about. Heck, it was only a Subaru.'

'He's lucky to have you for a mother.'

'Tell him that! Guess you'd be pretty mad if some kid of yours smashed up that car you've got, huh?'

Feeling the colour at his temples pale, Johannes is thankful for the darkness. 'It's only a car,' he says quickly. 'I've not had it long.'

'Uh-huh?'

'Two months. I bought it just before I left.'

'It's a nice car. That's something I miss, you know. Being able to buy something for yourself just 'cause you want it. Can't do that when you've got kids. Not that I was buying myself antique sports cars or anything 'fore I had Harley, but you know what I mean. You just can't do that with kids. Think hard before you have a family, Mr Professor.'

She holds up a finger to Johannes's silence in mock warning, then brushes her hand through the air.

'You make great parents though, Capricorns. Protectors, that's what you are. Comes naturally to wanna protect your loved ones. My Harle, he's Capricorn. It's like me, I'm Cancer. Cancers make good parents, too. Nurturers, that's what we are. I think about it sometimes, you know. Best thing I ever did with my life was having Harley. I mean, when I was young I never would have thought . . . I mean, who ever thinks they're gonna end up –' she pauses. 'Well, you know what I mean. But if I could go back, wouldn't change a thing. Not one thing. Because if one little thing changed, maybe I wouldn't have Harley. That's what it comes down to, isn't it?

'You want me to tell you something?' she says after some minutes. 'My name's not really Liza,' she says, and pauses. 'Church-christened Lisa, with an "s", but I changed it. About four years ago.'

'Why?'

''Cause I could,' her laugh comes loose once more then falters. 'Just 'cause I could.'

He nods. In the dense foliage of the mesquite bushes the cicadas perch. He listens to their noise again, their insistent rhythmic chirping.

'Guess I just wanted to show myself that things weren't fixed,' she says after a while. 'You know what I mean? That I've got some control over those . . . you know, like those basic things I just take for granted. That make any sense? I don't know. Guess I'd just come out of a relationship and I didn't want – I don't know kinda how to put this – didn't wanna feel as if I was just the same as when I went into it. I mean, course I wasn't the same, but . . . Guess I just wanted something definite to sort of show the *world* I wasn't the same person I'd been. Sound stupid?'

'No,' says Johannes, and shakes his head. And as he does, *Lisa Wales, Fairbank 1009* is the thought that comes into his mind. It saddens him for some reason he doesn't quite understand.

She swirls the wine in her glass and stares down in thought. 'You don't feel you've got control over life, do you?'

'Excuse me?'

'Just that,' she says simply, lifting her eyes from her glass. 'Just what I said. We don't have to talk about it.'

'No,' he says, quietly. She watches him a moment longer, then lowers her gaze again. After a few seconds Johannes reaches across the tabletop and, taking the wine bottle, fills his water glass almost to the rim. She doesn't look up, or if she does she doesn't say anything.

He should be used to waking in unfamiliar rooms by now, yet each time the sensation is still momentarily unsettling. This morning his head feels fugged. He's in a home, not a hotel, that much he can tell. There's an airbrushed poster of an underwater dolphin on one wall, a rust-coloured shag carpet, cork wall-panelling, and a brown-tiled en suite leading off from a doorway opposite the bed. Through the open window he can hear the lazy passing of suburban traffic. Arizona, he's in Arizona.

Lying beneath the sheet, in the already-hot air, the details of the previous evening begin to seep back into his consciousness.

Slowly at first, but then all of a sudden the evening's conclusion tumbles into focus.

'*Scheiße!*' Johannes murmurs, his eyes opening fully at the recollection. He struggles into an upright position, his hand nursing his forehead. '*Scheiße, scheiße, scheiße!*' She was drunk though, he acknowledges, with luck she'll have forgotten or dismissed it already.

As if on cue, a voice comes loudly from the hallway. It's moving rapidly down the corridor, accompanied by heavy steps. 'Are you insane, Mom?!' Johannes hears as the voice passes by his room. A door opens and slams.

'Harley,' comes Liza's voice, raised but more exasperated than angry, 'I have told you about slamming doors.'

A stereo has been turned on. Loudly. Johannes hears the thump-thump-thump of rock music – *Jefferson Airplane?* – passing through the wall behind the headboard of his bed.

'Harley, honey. I don't know why you're making such a big deal out of this.' Knocking. 'Harley, will you open up and talk to me? Honey? Open up, will you?'

Johannes pulls back the sheet and reaches for his clothes. He doesn't want to pretend he's still asleep. He wants to get his things together, get back in the car, and leave as soon as possible.

In the hallway he finds Liza sitting on the shag carpet against the opposite wall, knees pulled up to her chest. She looks very small and deflated. Around her shoulders is draped a purple blanket. She reminds him of the homeless women he's seen hanging out on Haight. The music still thumps from behind the closed door.

'Everything okay?'

She lifts her eyes. 'So, Harley came home,' she says with a pinched smile. 'Guess you heard, huh? We wake you?'

'No,' he says, with a shake of his head.

Liza just raises her eyebrows at him, disbelieving, then rests her head back against the wall. 'That kid, Jeez!' she shakes her head slowly from side to side.

'Liza –'

'Hey, I know it sounded bad but he's just strung out cause he's got his finals next month. That's all it is. He needs a bit of time to come round to the idea. But it's gonna be fine.'

'Look –'

'No really, he's a smart kid. He knows this isn't a chance you turn down. Free ride to Florida in an antique sports car? I mean, you gotta be kidding.' She leans one hand against the wall and heaves herself upright. 'I'll make us some breakfast,' she says as she walks past him to the kitchen.

'Florida,' is all Johannes can say in reply. Florida. A water glass full of wine on an empty stomach, and he offers to drive this woman and her son to Florida. It's a four-day drive at least. Four days there, four days back, and in between the Keys, and the palm trees, and all those animal parks she's so crazy about. He hears her in the kitchen, opening the fridge, reaching for pans. The boy's music travels clear through the thin walls. Johannes stands listening to it a moment longer in the door-frame, then turns to his room to shower and finally shave.

He has no idea what she says to persuade her son, but around noon the boy opens the door to his room and comes out with a duffle bag over one shoulder and a guitar across the other. 'I'm not gonna sit up back,' is all he says when he sees the car.

'I'll go in the rear. You take shotgun. Isn't it a great car, Harle?'

'Bet it doesn't have air conditioning.'

'It's a vintage car,' Johannes apologises.

'What are you talking about, you guys?' Liza protests. 'That car's got air conditioning. *Natural* air conditioning: windows roll down, don't they?' She shakes her head and steps away to load the trunk, leaving the two of them standing next to each other on the sidewalk. Johannes looks across at the boy but he's standing with his arms crossed, and doesn't acknowledge the glance.

He's not a bad-looking kid. His hair is long and sandy

blond, uncombed like his mother's. He's bigger than she is, with a youthful athletic build, like someone who might swim a lot. He looks healthy. Still only just on the verge of needing to shave. His T-shirt has a picture on it of a cross-legged Buddha. Dharma Meditation Camp, 1966, it says – the year Johannes was born. A pair of white headphones snake from his duffle bag and hang limp around his neck, while around one wrist he wears a bracelet of plaited string, woven with small shells and beads. He has the sort of pensive taciturnity and slow-wheeling eyes that most probably make long-haired high-school girls – the sort who fill notebooks full of poetry and dab patchouli behind their ears – dream about a boy like this.

'We should help,' says Johannes. The boy doesn't nod or say anything in return, but when the older man steps forward he follows him to the kerb.

They head east on Route 40. Outside Albuquerque they pull up at a gas station so Liza can buy water. Johannes watches her and Harley walking across the asphalt. She looks small next to her son. She's wearing leather sandals and saying something to him, even though the boy is still wearing the headphones he's had on since they left. Johannes watches them disappear into the store, and for a moment his thoughts turn to how easy it would be just to open his door, unload the trunk onto the sidewalk, and simply drive away. That easy to never see them again. They're not so far from home that they couldn't just find a bus station and catch a Greyhound back.

Earlier, as they pulled away from her street, Liza had reached from the back seat and touched Johannes's arm lightly. 'Here,' she said, holding out her palm, 'it'll protect us.' Johannes glanced down. In her hand lay a tiny chunk of pink-hued crystal. 'Put it on the dash,' she instructed. 'Rose quartz: protects when travelling, prevents accidents.'

The crystal sits now on the dashboard. There is a smokiness to its colour. Johannes stares at it a moment than reaches for it abruptly and drops it in the ashtray, pushing the little

hatch closed.

To unload their stuff and just drive away could be so easy right now.

Johannes closes his eyes, and waits for Liza and her son to return.

She talks a lot; he knew to expect that. The strange thing is, he finds he's growing to like it. The days pass with less torpor with her and Harley in the car.

'You know what I thought I was gonna do? With my life I mean?' She is leaning on the back of the passenger seat, one arm resting over her son's shoulder, dividing her attention between Johannes and the view through the windscreen. Harley is leaning against the passenger door, his arm resting on the window frame, eyes following the grey rush of the road. 'So, I was gonna be married with like five kids and I was gonna open an animal sanctuary. Uh-huh, that's what I thought.' She laughs. 'This is a long time ago. Way before I started studying the astrology. 'Fore I even had Harley. You know, like a big house with fields and fields all around – that's what I thought – and just cats and dogs and horses and . . . I'd take anything in. Tigers and chimps even, I guess. Are you laughing at me?'

'No,' says Johannes, laughing. 'Tigers?'

'You are laughing at me, aren't you? Don't laugh, I'm serious. Yeah, tigers. Tigers and chimps. Cheetahs. Look, I saw a TV show about this just last year. About rich people in LA and New York who are buying tiger cubs and baby chimpanzees 'cause they see them on TV and think they're cute. Then when they realise what they're dealing with they're throwing them onto the streets. You know, throwing chimpanzees onto the streets of LA. Don't laugh at me! I saw this on TV. Okay, so maybe it's not like chimps *all* over the streets of LA, maybe that was just one case. Whatever. They can all come stay at my sanctuary, sure. Stop laughing at me, will you? Haven't you ever had any animals?'

'A hamster,' says Johannes, smiling. 'Rolli. I gave him to the neighbour's child before I left.' He looks in the wing mirror and switches lanes.

'In San Francisco?'

'Yeah.'

'A hamster?'

'Yeah.'

'*A hamster?* Jeez!' She shakes her head, looking baffled, laughing. 'I so would not have put you a hamster person. Like a golden retriever maybe, but a hamster?'

'He wasn't really mine.'

'Oh my God, see that?' Liza interrupts. 'Look up front: Arkansas! It's the border sign!' She lets out a whoop of excitement. 'Harley, look at that, Harle, we're about to cross the Arkansas border.'

'I can see that for myself, Mom.'

'That's like, what, a thousand miles we've done? We must be over half way. Show a bit of excitement, Harley, baby.' She gives him a playful knock around the head.

'Fuck off, Mom,' he laughs.

'You asshole. Plug yourself back into your iPod. Don't kids just drive you crazy? I mean.'

There are fields surrounding them, wide yellow fields of sun-parched corn, and wind turbines lined on the horizon, their arms rotating in the pale blue sky. The road isn't busy, but cars pass, and trucks move steadily in the heat. Liza is still leaning forward in her seat, watching how the mirage of heat blurs the road up ahead. Her hair whips around her head from the airflow, and every few minutes she lifts an arm to push it from her face.

'So you ever miss your home?'

'Home here or –'

'No. Where you come from.'

'Sometimes.'

'Think you'll go back?'

'Not yet.' He catches his reflection in the rear-view mirror. Now his beard is gone, he looks again like how he remembers himself.

35

'You should tell me more about where you come from, you know. Is that where Heidi comes from?'

He laughs. 'That was Switzerland.'

'Switzerland, huh? There you go, see? Hey, can we pull over up here? I need to pee. Harley, you got my bag? Harley?'

That's how it goes as the miles and miles of road pass beneath them. The conversations in the car, and mealtimes at roadside diners with Liza complaining about how they serve fries with everything, and nights pulled over at motels when they each retire to their separate rooms. She does yoga in her room and meditates with the purple blanket over her shoulders. The boy plays his guitar, and sometimes Johannes can hear his playing through the wall. Sometimes he even thinks he hears singing. Melancholy, folky tunes that surprise him at first. It feels somehow intrusive to overhear something so raw and personal-sounding from one who says so little. In the days since they've left, though, Johannes has grown easier with the boy's silence. He sees it for habit now, rather than sullenness. There are even moments in the car, moments when Liza has fallen asleep and is finally quiet, when Johannes will look across to the boy and sometimes the two of them will catch each other's eye and half smile.

And then, on the fourth day, something changes. At breakfast, Johannes senses a coolness to Liza's manner that he can't explain. Her effervescence seems to have fallen flat.

'Where's the girl with the coffee?' she complains.

Johannes is looking at the map. 'I think we're only a day's drive away. We should cross into Florida tonight.'

'Great,' she says, without enthusiasm. 'Hey, could I please get some more coffee?' she calls as the waitress brushes by. Her smile at the waitress drops again as she turns back to Johannes. 'Whole 'nother day, huh? I'd forgotten how much driving there is to get to Florida. It's kind of cramped in the back of that car of yours.'

'We can take a break if you want. Continue on tomorrow.'

'No,' she sighs, 'I just wanna get there now.' She turns to stare out the window. There are trucks passing on the road before the restaurant.

Harley glances across at Johannes, keeps his eyes on him a moment, then turns back to his eggs.

'We'll get on after breakfast, then,' says Johannes.

Nobody says anything.

It's growing dark and he's still driving. He wants to cross the border before they stop for the night. Both Liza and Harley have fallen asleep and the car is quiet but for the rush of air through the windows. Liza's body is curled on the leather upholstery of the back seat, one leg pulled up by her chest, the other reaching across to the gap behind his seat. Her head, leaning back, looks more naked in sleep, the orange glow from the street lamps painting quickly across her cheek as they pass beneath each one. Harley has his head against the headrest, his mouth open slightly.

The day has been awkward, unpopulated by words, and Johannes is looking forward to sleep. His body is cramped from the long hours in the car. Things seem unreal again.

He thinks about the crystal in the ashtray. Flicking open the little hatch he sees it lying there. Incongruous in the small metal compartment, like a tiny meteorite fallen from the sky. It glints in the artificial shine of the street lamps. He glances down at it, then back to the road, then back down again.

'To protect you when travelling,' she had said of the small talisman. 'Prevent accidents.'

Johannes gently presses his foot on the accelerator and feels the Karmen Ghia's engine purr a little faster, the road begin to move more quickly beneath them. He steps down harder – still gently though – changes lanes to slip past a car in front, changes back again. The dial on the speedometer is creeping upwards with the pressure of his foot. Johannes holds the wheel more tightly. His passengers don't stir. He's never driven the car this fast before. The accelerator won't go any further. He slips the car into overdrive. Faster, faster. His jaw is firm, his eyes fixed upon the road before them. He's holding his breath, his chest tight. Weaving deftly between the traffic.

At that moment Johannes has the odd sensation of being somehow dislocated from his body, as if something else has taken control. His actions manoeuvre the car, but they feel purely instinctive, like he's on autopilot, like he's steering one of those arcade games on demo mode, where everything has been programmed for perfection. Nothing seems real. Even the other vehicles seem to have been choreographed to move out of his way on cue. He knows full well he's tempting fate, but something won't allow him to release the pedal.

Johannes glances into the rear-view mirror, and sees Liza still lost in sleep. The speedometer quivers at its limit, and finally, finally, Johannes lets loose the breath he's been holding.

In the ashtray lies the crystal.

He lets the car release. It begins to decelerate, and beyond the windows the world echoes. The sky is dark. As the engine eases, the needle on the speedometer gradually inches back until it comes to hover at a legal level. In their seats, the woman and her son are still asleep.

Johannes wipes at his eyes with the back of his hand and finds them wet with tears. He reaches to the ashtray, and in one smooth movement hurls the crystal from the open window.

Later that night, in the parking lot of a cheap motel just beyond Jacksonville, the boy comes up to Johannes as he's checking the tyre pressures.

'Hi,' says Johannes, glancing up briefly.

'Hey,' says the boy. He stands above him on the kerb, watching silently as Johannes returns to his task.

'She knows about your wife, you know,' he says eventually. 'And your kids.'

Johannes's head lifts.

'So were you gonna tell her?'

'She couldn't –'

The kid is frowning, when all of a sudden he releases a tired laugh. 'Oh, man, wait.' He laughs again and shakes his head. 'It's none of her psychic shit. Your passport is in the glove box, next of kin written in.'

'The passport,' sighs Johannes, leaning his forehead against his hand. His face is pale. 'She saw my passport.'

'Yeah.' Harley is quiet again, watching the older man. He waits a full minute or more for him to speak. 'You're kinda freaking me out, dude. You gonna say something?'

'I just thought you meant –' Johannes pauses. 'It doesn't matter, I'm sorry.'

'Hey look, all I'm saying, man, is –' he draws a breath, 'I don't care. I don't care what you've done. Who you've left. I don't care if you're sleeping with my mom even.'

'I'm not –'

'Look, man, I don't give a shit. All I'm saying is just don't fuck her up, okay?'

'It's not what you think, Harley.'

Harley stares at him for the longest time. 'Just don't fuck up my mom, okay?'

Johannes holds his gaze, then finally lets his eyes drop. He focuses on the boy's beaten-up sneakers. 'Capricorns,' she'd said, hadn't she? 'You protect your loved ones.'

'Okay,' says Johannes quietly.

He hears Harley turn, hears his steps retreat across the night-time parking lot.

On the way back to his room, just a step or two from his door, Johannes falters and doubles back on himself. Low-down and quietly, he knocks on her bedroom door.

'Harley?' he hears, her voice sleep-thick. 'That you?'

'Liza?' he says quietly.

'John? Door's not locked.' As he pushes the door, he sees her elbowing herself up in the bed and reaching for the lamp switch. 'John?' Her eyes squint tightly against the unexpected light as she looks across to him in the doorframe. 'Something wrong?'

He shakes his head, but still she frowns.

'You need something?'

'Can I come in?'

She looks confused, her eyes still childish, unaccustomed to the light. 'Sure,' she says.

He dreams of that night he came home late, the night he'd been out at a bar with a student, drinking white wine. He dreams of how he slid his key into the lock of their house on Russian Hill, sandwiched on that steep street between other buildings, each one completely different from the next. It was a summer night, one of those early-summer nights when the sky stays light for the longest time, violet-hued. Inside, the lights were out, but it wasn't so dark that he couldn't see without them. Everything was blue-tinged, ghostly – the white walls, the stripped wood floors – it was like being inside an old television set. The house was absolutely silent. As he walked up the corridor, he could see the girls' paintings on the kitchen wall flapping in the night breeze. She'd left the french doors open again. He'd told her about that, about leaving the doors open when she wasn't in the room, because even though the outside deck was enclosed, this was America, and in America you never know. He slid the doors shut and locked the catch, then dropped his keys on the table and his jacket over the back of a dining chair. He ran himself a glass of water, and drank it standing at the counter-top. A cold drip trickled slowly down his wrist.

The door to the girls' room on the landing upstairs was open. They lay sprawled asleep in their bunks, neat in their flowered pyjamas, their two small faces pink and sleep-flushed, hair ruffled. As he watched over them, a faint rattling noise broke the silence. In the hamster cage, Rolli began to run in his wheel.

The windows in the bedroom were open and the curtains undrawn. They billowed and sank in the cool night air.

40

Moonlight silvered the room. His wife was lying on the covers, her back to him, her breathing gentle. She was still fully dressed, as if she'd just lain down for a moment and fallen asleep like that.

'Liesbeth,' he said, curling his body against hers, running his arm around her waist.

She murmured sleepily, shifted against him.

This family. How unbearably he loved them.

He held in his arms the soft rise and fall of her sleeping body, kissed the warm nape of her neck. He was slightly drunk. Only slightly.

The student he'd been drinking with; nothing had happened. Nothing ever would have happened. But still, when he closed his eyes that night, he saw her face, imagined her slowly removing her clothes for him.

Would it have been different if he'd known he had only a week left to protect them? That the ashtray of the family car was empty?

Johannes wakes in the dawn of a Florida motel room, lying on a patterned nylon bedspread, and reaches for the woman lying under the sheets beside him. He holds her tightly, feeling her body in his arms. 'I'm sorry,' he whispers against her chest.

Through her cotton nightdress she feels the hot warmth of his tears. 'It's okay,' she soothes. 'It's okay, honey.' She strokes at his hair. Kisses his forehead, softly as a mother might. 'Sweetheart, it's okay.'

The cars in line are funnelled down an alley of palm trees to reach the cash desk, stopping and starting until it comes their turn to pull up beside the kiosk. A pony-tailed girl in a yellow polo shirt smiles from the counter, 'Welcome to the Parrot Jungle!' she says over the intercom.

Liza is leaning forward as they drive up to the parking area, her elbows resting on the back of their seats. The path is lined with giant billboard cartoon parrots, smiling koalas, grinning

41

chimps. From her ear lobes dangle moonstones. 'God, it hasn't changed at all. You remember it, Harle?'

'Yeah,' says the boy, and despite himself smiles.

When they climb out of the car, she practically runs. 'Come on,' she is calling. 'I wanna show you something.' She turns to gesture for them to hurry, her skirt swaying about her legs.

'She's like a kid.'

'I like it,' says Johannes.

Harley seems to think about this. 'Yeah.'

They pass families with babies in strollers, children licking at ice creams, holding stuffed parrots under their arms. The ground is gravelled, a dusty red, but all around are palm trees, and other tropical bushes and plants and elaborate waterfalls constructed from giant fibreglass boulders. Birds are everywhere: flamingoes standing in man-made ponds, reflecting pink against the water; rainbow-hued parrots perching in the trees; storks balanced on one leg in the reeds; cockatiels and parakeets and canaries wheeling free in the sky above.

They pass a mini-arena in which a crowd cheers as a green parrot rides a unicycle back and forth along a tightrope.

But she doesn't stop. She's leading them to a double-gated entryway surrounded by a high net-topped fence. She pushes the first gate for them, then swings open the second.

It's even more lush, more verdant in here than on the other side. The air is humid from the dense foliage. Songbirds trill. Everywhere they look the sky is filled with tiny jewel-bright tropical birds and the flutter of butterflies. It's like a dream. The wings of the butterflies dust past their eyelids, the trail of tail feathers sweeps their shoulders.

'Isn't it beautiful? Isn't it just beautiful?'

She pulls her son into her embrace, and for a second her eyes close, then Johannes watches as they open wide again, as if she can't drink her fill of all that surrounds them.

'It's just so damn beautiful,' she says, her voice almost a whisper.

Caro at the Pool

SHE FOUND HER AT THE SWIMMING POOL. Caroline was lying on a sun-lounger in a pale green bikini, wearing yellow-rimmed sunglasses. One leg was pulled up towards her chest, a hand around the ankle. She held a bottle of Coke in the other hand, an orange straw reaching from the rim. Her hair wasn't exactly wet, but still curled a little damply at her neck. It looked very blonde in the sunlight. She was talking to a man on the sun-lounger beside her, waving her Coke bottle in the air as she described something, the bent straw swaying back and forth. He was laughing. He also wore sunglasses and held a bottle of Coke, no straw. He was leaning on one elbow, wearing a pair of blue trunks and had a birthmark shaped like an acorn on the skin just below his ribcage.

'Caroline!' She yelled out so loudly that several of the others around the pool also looked over momentarily. A small dog began to bark. Caroline lifted her sunglasses to look across, her mouth open, her body registering annoyance before she even recognised Hilary.

'Bloody hell,' she sighed, letting her glasses fall back to the bridge of her nose. She leant forward in her seat, one foot dropping to the ground as she did so. 'Go away!' she mouthed soundlessly.

'Caro-line!' Hilary called again, lifting one hand and curling her fingers through the wire of the fence.

Caroline shrugged her shoulders at the man beside her and said something Hilary couldn't hear. She dropped the other foot to the ground and slipped her sandals on as she passed her drink across to him, then walked over to Hilary very slowly, skirting the pool and pushing her glasses up on her head to hold her hair back from her face. '*Lord*,' she said as she reached Hilary, 'what in hell are you doing here?' She stood a little way back from the fence, her hands on her hips, one leg bent.

Hilary looked down at the grass, scratching at the ground with the toe of her plimsoll, her weight drooping from her hold on the wire. She was wearing a yellow sundress, the cotton clinging to her hot back. 'Mum and Dad sent me. I've been looking for you for almost *two* hours, you know. You're to come home and do your homework.' The rubber edging of her shoe was dusty with dry earth.

Caroline rolled her eyes and made a sound through her teeth, '*Rrrrr*.' She shifted her hips so the other leg bent, let out a sigh. 'Bloody hell, they think I'm a baby. I'm almost sixteen years old, for God's sake.'

Hilary was thirsty. She'd disturbed an ants' nest. The tiny creatures were scurrying through the dirt. One jerked its way across her toe and she shook her foot to dislodge it. 'Is that Mr James you're with?' she questioned, not looking up.

'Is it any of your business?' asked Caroline sharply. She turned and walked away from the fence.

'Caroline, you better come now,' called Hilary, her chin lifting. 'I'm waiting for you.'

Ignoring her sister, Caroline stopped at the edge of the pool and flipped off her sandals, then folded her sunglasses and placed them on the ground. She didn't look back to the man, simply tugged with her fingers at the elastic hem of her bikini top, pulling it further below her breasts, then stretched her arms high and dived neatly into the pool. She swam a length, a precise fast crawl, turned in the water and returned to the side. Hair slick against her head, she lifted herself easily from the pool. Again she tugged at her bikini top before replacing her sunglasses and sandals.

Only now did she turn to smile at the man.

'Caroline,' Hilary shouted behind her as Caroline walked slowly back to her sun-lounger. The man held up her Coke and she took it but didn't sit back down. She drank what was left in the bottle, her lips pursed about the orange straw, until the last drops gurgled. She wrinkled her nose at the man and laughed.

'I've got to go.' She gestured her head wearily towards the fence. 'My sister.'

'I know,' he said, looking across to the young girl.

Caroline nodded absently. She picked up her towel and hung it across her arm. 'See you Monday, then.' She turned.

'Monday.' He lifted his hand, caught her leg, fingers resting for a fraction of a second in the crook of her knee. 'Goodbye, Caro.'

She looked back and smiled. 'Bye.' Caroline watched the surface of the water as she walked back to the changing cubicles. It shimmered brightly, catching the light, she thought, in a way that looked almost like a sound too high to hear.

The Ocularist's Wife

THERE IS A CERTAIN POINT IN THE DAY, LATE afternoon – the exact hour dependent upon the season – when, if the sun might happen to shine, the walls of Monsieur Hervé P. Pontellier's establishment light up iridescent. Those small orbs that line each shelf are set aglow and the very air is shot with jewel-like colour. Sitting at his desk, Monsieur Pontellier will lift his head and pause. Across his face, the rainbow shimmer of a live trout slipping from the hands.

Passing in the corridor behind the shop, as she steps to retrieve a forgotten novel from the garden, the glowing rectangle of light pulls at Madame Pontellier's attention. She turns her head, the tendons in her pale neck curving smoothly into line with her shoulder blade. The corridor is dark and the tunnelled effect of the lighted doorway in the distance reminds her of looking down a child's kaleidoscope, the way the colours slot gently back and forth amongst themselves like dancers on a ballroom floor. Softly, her weight rests back upon the silken heels of her slippers, feet still paced apart on the tiles.

Her husband's back is angled from her while his face, raised to bask in the light, is held in profile.

He is a large man, Monsieur Pontellier, a man whose knees

51

graze the underside of his desktop. He carries his size awkwardly, as if it embarrasses him somewhat. Standing upright, his head hangs forward a little, shoulders droop backwards, legs are loosely angled at the knee. He almost has the concertina profile of someone seen in a fairground mirror. The distorted glass has further stretched his facial features too, for forehead and chin recede backwards behind the length of his nose, their diagonals hampered only by the sweep of his hairline and the jut of his Adam's apple. He has no chin to speak of. Keeping his arms close at his sides, his tread is careful, like one walking anxious through a tightly packed china shop. He gives the appearance of a man constantly wary of clumsy movement, which is strange, because Monsieur Pontellier is by nature extremely precise.

The bell at the door breaks his contemplation.

'Ah ha,' says his visitor, gesturing towards those luminous spheres surrounding them, 'the eyes of heaven look upon us today!'

Pontellier chuckles, 'Afternoon, Courtois.'

'Good afternoon to you, too,' says Courtois, taking a seat at the desk, his feet lifting to perch on the stool's rungs. 'Spectacular, ha, quite spectacular,' he revolves his head in the tinted light. 'You could charge a franc entry to see this, my friend.'

'I daresay. And how does the day treat you, Courtois?'

'Oh, quite fine, quite fine. The marmoset is pregnant.'

'The marmoset?' Pontellier cocks his head.

'The marmoset, indeed. Quite a coup. Terribly difficult to breed in captivity.' He crosses one leg over the other then studies a skim of dirt lodged beneath his fingernails.

'I see, yes I see.' Pontellier is working while he talks. Fashioning a perfect pupil, flecking pale threads of paint across an azure iris.

He has known Courtois, the city zookeeper, since their schooldays. Still remembers him a boy with eager voles in his pockets and newts squirming in his handkerchief.

Perhaps because his career has indulged his childhood passion, Courtois has retained a youthfulness of appearance. His skin still blooms pink at the cheeks and his hair is parted neatly and combed flat as if by an attentive matriarch. He has an endearing habit of blinking his eyelids rapidly, a quiver of lash beneath the thick lenses of his spectacles. There are always, to his great irritation, short mammalian hairs caught in the wool of his suits which even persistent brushing seems unable to remove. His appearance is otherwise meticulous.

Before Pontellier, Courtois assumes a languid air of articulate confidence, but it is a quality he finds himself unable to reproduce before other men. 'Lord, what heat,' he sighs, drawing a mustard-coloured handkerchief from his pocket (no newts these days) and wiping it across his forehead. 'I suppose you've read the newspaper?'

Squinting at his brush strokes, Pontellier's response is solemn. 'They're goading us with that dispatch.'

'My view exactly.'

'And I've a fear we might take the bait.' He worries at his lower lip a moment and draws in a deep breath, his nostrils flaring. 'Lord help us if we do, that's all I can say.'

'Lord help us? You don't think we'd win?' All of a sudden, Courtois's attention is distracted by a slight movement in the corner and he stumbles to his feet. 'Madame Pontellier,' he says politely, dipping his head, the brilliantine upon his hair glinting in her direction.

Madame Pontellier has the pale constitution of a woman in the early stages of consumption. The disease is merely nibbling at present, gnawing slightly from within; so quiet that it goes as yet undetected, mistaken for that only vaguely unhealthy apathy not irregularly the preserve of well-bred young ladies with time on their hands. She spends the afternoons reclining upon the chaise longue, a romance splayed at her side, the pages barely turned, her eyelids fluttering weakly at the edges of sleep. The maid treads quietly so as not to disturb her mistress, removes a cup of tepid tea, careful not to let the cup rattle in the saucer, and thinks to herself, 'Why, no wonder she lacks colour.'

Madame Pontellier stands now in the doorway, very slightly off centre, her gaze level. She is the colour of porcelain. With a faint nod, she acknowledges Courtois.

'Supper, Hervé,' she says. 'If you'll come up now to wash, please.' She slides her eyes back to the zookeeper. 'Good evening, Monsieur Courtois,' and bows her head a fraction.

The two men are silent as she turns, listening to the dry whisper of her skirts against the tiles.

Courtois draws in his breath with a faint sucking sound, 'Madame calls. I'd better let you go, heh?' He is still fumbling with his hat brim, feigning jocularity. 'Until tomorrow?'

'Until tomorrow.' Pontellier watches his friend leave and notices that the evening sun has passed. His shop has submerged once again in dusty shade and those false eyes lining the walls are cold and hard.

20th of July 1870

Knowing that his friend doesn't step out until lunchtime to buy the daily newspaper, Courtois denies himself his morning coffee to pay a fleeting visit to Pontellier's shop. He walks the streets briskly in the early sun, the news folded beneath his arm, perspiration causing the print to smudge against his jacket front. But it is not Monsieur Pontellier whom he finds behind the counter when he pushes open the door but Madame.

She is sitting in her husband's chair, idly flicking through a fashion journal laid on the desk before her. She looks up when Courtois enters and arches her eyebrows. 'Monsieur Courtois, what brings you here so early?'

Courtois has come to a surprised halt before the desk. He drops his head and finds himself looking at the widespread page of her magazine. Pen and ink renderings of women's corsetry, the models cut below the torso, trussed at the bosom, beribboned, their backs arching, their lips open slightly as if

54

the garments leave them silently gasping for breath. Madame Pontellier's gaze drops with his, stares flatly at the fashion spread, lifts again. 'Can I help you, Monsieur Courtois?'

He falters, 'I was looking for . . .'

'Hervé's out back, blowing glass.' She gestures towards the rear of the house. 'Of course, I could disturb him for you.'

Her voice, thinks Courtois, is like spilt liquid creeping across floorboards. He feels obliged to decline her offer, assuring her instead that, 'Oh no, no, it's nothing important. Certainly nothing of any urgency.' And then, adding almost as an afterthought, 'Only, perhaps you might be so kind as to ensure that he sees this,' and he thrusts the creased and sweaty newspaper across the countertop.

As he finishes, the door opens behind him. Courtois swivels his body towards the entering customer with palpable relief: a corpulent gentleman with a black felt eyepatch, the arrival of whom provides the necessary distraction for Courtois to take his leave without ceremony.

The gentleman approaches the counter, wheezing in the heat, and leans towards Madame Pontellier. 'Morning, Madame.' He is a fleshy-lipped man of ruddy complexion. 'Cecil Bouillot. I was having an *eye* custom-made.' A fleck of spittle lands upon the newspaper lying between them. 'Would it be ready for collection, do you know?'

With a neat movement, Madame Pontellier closes the page of her magazine upon Courtois's paper and sweeps it aside.

'Bouillot? One moment.' A row of small brown paper envelopes is pinned against the wall, their lower halves each a pregnant bulge beneath a pencilled name. Madame Pontellier runs her finger along the line, reciting the names as she does so. 'Guyot-Clement, Courtillon, Ducasse . . . *Bouillot*.' She pinches the pin from the wall and tips out the contents of the envelope. 'Monsieur, if you please,' she says politely, lifting her hand before him. Bouillot squints his good eye at the glassy replica lying still in Madame Pontellier's palm. With a tremor, his fat lips lift into a smile.

55

'Ah, Madame.' He exhales slowly. 'Incredible! Your husband is a genius.'

Madame Pontellier reaches the fingers of her other hand to play at the corner of her mouth.

'May I?' questions Bouillot, reaching already like a child for a bonbon. He twists the little sphere between his heavy fingers. 'May I try it?'

Before she can nod assent, he has flipped back the eyepatch to reveal a pinkened clump of flesh bunched about a dark cavity. A small muscle in disarray causes the tissue to jerk rapidly as if alive. Bouillot pops the orb into the hollow, smiles with satisfaction to feel how the skin suckers close about the cool glass.

Like a greedy sea anemone, thinks Madame Pontellier, her stomach curdling faintly with distaste.

She hands a small mirror across to him and watches as he fingers the glass surface of the eye to align the iris with its azure counterpart. The muscle beneath the glassy curve still twitches erratically. 'Fantastic, ha. Quite fantastic. A remarkable match, don't you think, Madame?' asks Monsieur Bouillot without turning from the mirror.

Bouillot departs shortly, leaving congratulations for Monsieur Pontellier, money for the cash till, and a black felt eyepatch for the wastebasket. As the shop door springs closed behind him, Madame Pontellier drops back into her husband's seat and draws her hands up to cover her face, her fingertips pressing against her closed eyelids. She remains like this for several moments before taking a deep breath and blinking her eyes open, then reaches for her magazine and slides it across the countertop. Opening it, her gaze falls on Courtois's newspaper. She turns it to read the headline: *FRANCE DECLARES WAR*. Her eyes scan the cover article slowly, a frown creasing her forehead, until Madame Pontellier's head lifts and she finds herself lost in a memory of a spring holiday she once took in Prussia as a child.

Monsieur Pontellier likes his meat rare. Likes to take a slice into his tournedos and watch the blood ooze colour into the pale of the pepper sauce. Likes to taste the animal in what he eats. And he needs this now, needs a delight in something simple to divert his attention.

They are seated at the dining table, Pontellier in his house slippers, his shirt collar loosened. The blinds have been drawn to shield the afternoon sun and it is almost dark in the room but for fine slants of light that eke below the tasselled trim. The air is stuffy. Madame Pontellier sits across the table from her husband, dressed in light green silk, the colour reflecting dully upon her cheekbones. Her dark hair is pulled sharply back from her face and pinned neatly in place by an ivory comb. She is breathing in quick shallow breaths through her mouth, her eyes flickering about the room, darting past her husband's form so as she shan't catch his gaze should he look up.

'An excellent piece of beef, my dear,' he declares finally, wiping his napkin across his mouth. Reaching for his newspaper, he shakes it open before him. Feels once again the slight stirring within him of a sensation akin – he can't deny it – to nervous exhilaration. Pontellier knows already of exactly what he will read; current events have become too precipitate to wait until lunchtime. Each one of his morning's customers has entered with the news skittering on their lips, wanting to discuss and argue, needing words to give shape to reality. The city is alive with the changes taking place around and within it, its consciousness heightened by the accelerated pace of all that is occurring – from another military defeat at war and the surrender of their emperor has come a bloodless revolution, the effortless overturning of an empire. All so fast. In the moment before he begins to read, his glance lifts briefly above the page.

Madame Pontellier's eyes have fallen suddenly still. Her face has assumed an expression of composed lethargy. It is an expression her husband recognises with some weariness. Her plate is barely touched.

'Is something wrong?' He peers across his newspaper, features pointed with dutiful concern.

'I don't have an appetite,' sighs Madame Pontellier, sliding the plate further from her.

Pontellier hesitates, wondering whether he should pass around the table to put an arm about her, decides against it. 'Are you sickening?' He lowers his paper. 'You have been looking a trifle peaky of late. Should we call the doctor perhaps?'

'Hervé, *no* . . .' her voice trails. 'I simply haven't an appetite today. Do stop fussing.' She rises from her seat, dropping her napkin against the tablecloth, and crosses to the chaise longue.

Monsieur Pontellier gazes awkwardly at the remains of her meal; the salad turning limp in the heat, the skin forming on the pepper sauce.

'Perhaps, perhaps a jargonelle.' She speaks from beneath closed eyelids.

'A jargonelle? A *pear*, you mean?'

'A jargonelle,' she sounds the word with accentuated precision.

'Of course,' he sighs, 'a jargonelle. I'll ask Claudine.' He folds his paper and exits to find the maid. Without opening her eyes, Madame Pontellier begins to fan herself slowly with one hand. Her foot has fallen in a shaft of light and she curls it into the shadow back towards herself, kicking off the shoe as she does so and digging her stockinged heel into a cool crack in the upholstery. She waits like this for her husband to return. When he does he tells her, as she knew he would, that there aren't any jargonelles in the house. He'll step out to try and find one for her.

'Wait!' she cries, as he turns at the door. 'Will you come here, please, Hervé?' He crosses and lowers himself beside her. She still has her eyes closed, but smiles a little, a slim smile, a smile that barely exerts, as he begins to stroke at her temple. 'Do you love me?' she asks in a level voice.

Gently, he smoothes a stray lock of hair pressed against the damp of her brow.

'Let's go away . . .' her lips are dry, '. . . take a holiday.'

'It's hardly the best of times for a holiday, my love.' His hand has fallen still. The moment makes him feel suddenly awkward, too long of limb to be crouching like this.

'We could go to the Alps.'

'Let's just wait and see, heh? See what happens with this war.'

'That war, Hervé, it won't affect *us*, will it?' She frowns beneath his fingertips.

He pauses before continuing slowly, 'No. No, my darling. We're sure to see victory any day now.' He is glad she hasn't opened her eyes. In the dim light he studies her calm features, wondering if she can truly be that unaware of everything beyond herself. 'Don't you worry,' he says softly, 'this war shan't affect you in the least.'

'Then I don't care to think on it.'

Again, he is made to pause. A frown now smocks his brows as he observes her. 'I'll fetch your jargonelle, my dear,' he says abruptly. Leaning, he plants a kiss upon her cheek and has to halt himself from overbalancing.

She lies as she is until she hears the front door shut closed behind him, then wipes at her cheek with the back of her hand and rises. Her meal is still sitting on the table, the knife and fork pointing expectantly towards the rim of the plate. She lifts the meat between thin fingers and reaches her mouth towards it, careful not to let the sauce drip onto the silk of her dress. 'My silly darling,' she says aloud between mouthfuls. 'Did I forget to tell you this isn't the season for jargonelles?'

11th of November 1870

The scuffle of wings is what awakens her; a pigeon has landed on the windowsill. Scratching the claws of one foot against the wood, it arcs its head back into its feathers, its bill reaching and teasing at some small parasite. A pitiful creature, skinny with dull matted feathers, gnarled legs deformed. The bird brings its head back up for air, bobbing its neck and shaking its wings again. Around the eyes, some disease has balded the skin to an angry pink.

'Shoo!' calls Madame Pontellier sharply, realising how long it is since she last saw a bird. The creature declines to stir. Irritated now, Madame Pontellier steps up from the chaise longue and across to the window, clapping her hands to make the pigeon flee. It spreads its wings and launches itself from the sill.

A lanky sallow-skinned youth has been watching the bird from the street. As it flies off he runs desperately after it, a hessian sack flapping in his hand. Madame Pontellier watches as the bird lifts into the white sky, then turns back to the drawing room. Her book has fallen face down onto the carpet but she doesn't reach to retrieve it, nor does she tidy the blanket which trails from the seat. The clock on the mantelpiece ticks with a quiet regularity.

'I'll go out,' she says suddenly, speaking aloud into the empty room. 'Yes, I'll go out,' she says again, this time more firmly. And, having made the decision, she realises she must move herself quickly before lassitude overtakes once more. She strides through to the bedroom, the swirl of her skirts behind her disturbing the maid kneeling to polish the parquet. Claudine looks up, her neck craning to follow her mistress. She is surprised at such uncharacteristic haste.

'Something is wrong, Madame?' she asks tentatively, leaning forward on her polishing rag to catch a better view.

She sees Madame Pontellier in front of the dressing table, hairpins clamped between her lips as she rearranges her hair. Lifting her chin upwards, she tilts her head from side to side, her eyes fixed on the looking glass. At one point she pauses and stares coldly at her own reflection, the intensity unsparing as if she is seeing for the first time a stranger and trying to memorise the face. A second later she stretches to reach for a hat perched on a mahogany stand behind her. It is a wide-brimmed raven-coloured affair, an ostrich feather bowing from the brim. Only now does she acknowledge Claudine.

'Lace my boots, please, Claudine.'

'Of course, Madame,' chimes the girl, scurrying up from her knees and smoothing her apron as she comes into the room. 'The grey boots, Madame?'

Lowering her eyelids briefly in agreement, Madame Pontellier extends one foot towards the maid and rests back in her seat. And at that very moment it simply leaves her again, the desire to go out – how *comfortable* this little chair is – she actually feels it leaving, seeping from her toes into the pattern of the carpet, slipping from her fingers down the velvet arms of the chair. The recognition rankles. 'How can you be so slow?' she asks irritably, ignoring the obvious hurry with which the girl is weaving the laces tight about the boot hooks.

'Is Madame going *out*?' queries Claudine as she ties the second lace, her tone somewhat incredulous.

And with that it is back, the yearning to leave the house, to escape the thick air of the drawing room. She sweeps up from her seat and steps fast from the room, her words crackling behind her, 'Madame certainly is. Tell my husband, if you please, that I'll return before supper.'

'Shouldn't I go with you?' calls Claudine hopelessly.

Seated back upon her heels, the maid watches her mistress's departure, follows the blood-red silk of her dress disappearing from the doorframe, and the last oily flash of that dandling ostrich feather.

'Well, I'll be . . .' she murmurs to herself and rises, rubbing at her stiff knees as she does so.

In the street, Madame Pontellier feels suddenly very alone, so unused is she to stepping out without a companion. It makes her strangely conscious of her physical being, of where her skin stops and the rest of the world begins. There are brittle autumn leaves caught at her feet which are sent whirling along the pavement by an impulsive squall of wind. She inhales the afternoon into her lungs, relishing the chill in the air, the hint of damp. Not that the day is altogether dull. The sky is papered with dense grey clouds but these are splitting at the seams like a piece of silk wearing thin and the late-afternoon light is easing through each snaking divide. It reflects against the glassy shopfronts, lighting them up like a row of teeth.

Madame Pontellier releases her breath slowly, then inhales again, her chest rising as she does so. Keeping her mouth tight, she lifts one hand and presses her palm against the doorframe, as if to test its solidity. Surprised at how the wood resists the pressure of flesh and bone, she releases the breath.

The colours are what catch at the corner of her eye. The lucidity of them. And turning, she sees her husband, seated at his work desk, surrounded by the glimmer of light through coloured glass. There is a quality of containment about the scene, framed as it is within the neat rectangle of his shop window, a neatly printed sign stating *Business as Usual* running like a subtitle along its lower half. It has a sense of composure, like a stage set for a ballet or the tiny perfection of a small room in a doll's house. Pontellier hasn't seen her. He is hunched over the wooden desktop, peering at a glass eyeball held between his fingertips. His brush moves like the tongue of a snake, quick darts that fleck the glass minutely. The movement is echoed subconsciously on his face in the twitching and pursing of his lips, the pleating of his brows.

There is something very charming in observing an individual so absorbed, so oblivious to anything beyond themselves. From her vantage in the street, Madame Pontellier feels the low thrill of the voyeur. She is transfixed.

How strange it is, that he should seem to her so utterly familiar and yet almost unrecognisable. When did the skin of his forehead begin the slow inching back of his hairline? When did those creases form around his eyes? She feels a sudden surge of warmth for her husband. A desire to take the curve of his head in her hands and kiss those shining expanses of skin at his temples. To rest her mouth a moment in the shallow dip of each eye socket, feeling the lashes batting like a moth beneath her lips. To trace the contours of his cheeks with the tip of her tongue.

And it is then that she notices: the glassy illumined eyes upon the walls are staring at her. Every single one of them. Staring fixedly in absolute silence.

With a gasp, Madame Pontellier turns and slams smack into an unexpected obstruction.

'Oh!' she cries. 'Oh! Monsieur Courtois!'

'Madame Pontellier,' he catches her shoulder to hold her upright, 'whatever's wrong?'

'Oh, my,' she lifts her hand to her neck and clutches at her collar. 'Please, I'm quite fine. I . . . I was merely going to take a walk,' she falters.

'A walk? Now? Alone?' There is a subtle hint of scorn underlying his bemusement.

'Yes,' she says faintly.

'And Monsieur Pontellier knows about this? Madame, don't you realise that it's not *safe* for you to walk out alone? It could be dangerous, extremely dangerous. The city is under *siege*, Madame.'

His manner surprises her more than his words, so used is she to his awkward reserve. And now that she looks at him, how curious, the man is almost transformed. Deep furrows have been drawn across his brow. Wan smudges swim beneath his heavy spectacle lenses where the skin below his eyes has puffed a shining mauve. His cheeks have lost their bloom, covered instead now by a rough shadow of stubble. His dark hair is in disarray.

She steps back from his hold. 'You're quite right, Monsieur Courtois,' she says carefully, 'I don't know what I was thinking.' Although she smiles, she feels a tightness in her chest, the resurfacing of an anxiety which, for a moment, she can't explain. 'Come, let us go in together.'

And as he steps to take her arm he dips his left hand, retrieving a brown-paper-wrapped package dropped in the collision.

It has the limp quality of a butcher's parcel. She looks down briefly, but is distracted as they approach the shopfront. Confronted once again by those staring glass eyes, Madame Pontellier recalls suddenly the cause for her underlying sense of alarm.

14th of December 1870

'Please come to the table and eat, Mireille,' pleads Monsieur Pontellier.

'One moment,' Madame Pontellier says irritably, without turning from the window.

Outside, the snow is falling thickly, veiling the small procession trailing below in the street. There are five figures in the party. Slow-moving silhouettes, like vertical pen marks on a white page. The two in front are wheeling a small funeral cart, steam spreading from their nostrils and mouths and rising white into the grey sky. The corpses on the cart are laid neatly – only two this time, but one of them short, a child perhaps. The stomachs bloat beneath the blankets, forming small humps which the mantle of snow accentuates. The street is otherwise deserted. Hushed. Curlicued wrought-iron balconies lean silently out from the façades like crouching dark skeletons.

'It's almost beautiful,' says Madame Pontellier quietly. Her breath mists against the cold glass.

'What's that you said?'

'Nothing, my darling,' she murmurs as she slides sideways into her seat, one leg folded beneath her. She lifts her fork and spins it slowly between her fingers as she regards her casserole.

There is a knock on the door. They both look over to see Claudine enter. 'Monsieur Courtois is here to see you, sir,' she says.

As Pontellier rises the maid bobs her head and ducks out again. Courtois is hanging back in the dim hallway. 'Come in,' urges Pontellier.

'I've disturbed your lunch,' says Courtois apologetically. 'I should come back later,' but he remains as he is, poised in the hallway.

'Nonsense.' Pontellier gestures again for his friend to enter. 'Please come in.'

Awkward, Courtois hovers on the threshold, his eyes darting over the dinner table.

'Afternoon,' says Madame Pontellier, still twisting her fork in her fingers. 'Join us, if you wish, Monsieur Courtois, we've plenty,' she says plainly, mistaking the preoccupation of his gaze for hunger.

'I'd rather not,' he rushes. 'Thank you all the same.'

Recognising his friend's distress, Pontellier rises and touches Courtois's arm gently. 'Would you prefer that we go downstairs?'

At Courtois's pained nod, he excuses them both and they leave Madame Pontellier in the room alone.

'Well, well, well,' she says, and stabs at a chunk of meat. After a few bites she lets her fork drop against the plate rim, spattering gravy onto the tablecloth, and stands up from the table.

It is just then, as she steps across the room, that her legs simply give way beneath her and Madame Pontellier collapses to the carpet. The shock of it winds her. She is utterly surprised, quite unsure at first if this could have been an action she had willed without realising it or whether something is actually wrong. She finds she is able to move her legs, but they feel clumsy, as if weights have been strung upon them. She doesn't get up. Waits instead to see if her fall has been heard by anyone.

She is close enough to smell the dusty wool of the carpet, to feel it prickle against her cheeks. Across the surface of its pattern, if she half-closes her eyes, it looks almost like a field of parched flowers, all pressed up against one another. She lets her eyes drift back across the surface of the carpet and again breathes in the sweetly arid smell of the wool. Without purpose, she dips the tip of her tongue from her mouth and, very slowly, runs it over the rug.

No one has come to find her. She notes this suddenly and feels a bristle of annoyance. Raising herself, she twists her body round into a seated position. Her fingers lift to her mouth to pick at minuscule flecks of carpet fibre that have caught on her tongue. She wipes them afterwards on her dress front, then rearranges the pins in her hair. The maid should be called to clear the table, she thinks, heaving herself up to exit the room.

It is as she passes the stairwell that she hears the low murmur of their voices. She can't hear any words, just a sonorous lilt of distant sound. Only as she moves quietly down the wooden stairs does the sound begin to clarify, to break itself into distinct words and phrases. She doesn't even listen to the meaning, she is hearing only the rhythm and pattern of their speech, almost as though she were listening to a piece of music.

'I don't know what to do, Pontellier. I don't know how to pass the hours any more.'

'Look, it can't last much longer.'

'And when it does end, if it ever does? What then? What do I have left?'

'You can't think like that.'

'How else can I think? I've lost everything. Good God, how could I have let this happen?'

'Quiet now . . . you *had* to do it, it wasn't a choice – people are starving in the streets.'

'But I'm not helping *them*.'

'You can't help them all.'

His laugh is wry. 'One evening last week, coming home, I passed one of those restaurants. The bright lights gaudy in the deserted street. A quartet playing a lively waltz that turned my soul, a very devil's dance it sounded to me. And there, at the glowing windows, I watched them in their finery. Laughing, joking, smacking lips glossy with grease. I turned away and retched onto the street.' Neither man says anything for a moment. 'That's who I'm "helping", Pontellier. That's who. Society dames with their diamonds still looped around their necks, overweight lords chewing on their cigar ends, feyly poking at their dinner plates. And they, who have the privilege to dine on such "delicacies", have the gall to jest – I've heard them – quipping that only the talent of our Parisian chefs could have made such "quaint" dishes palatable – it makes me sick.'

'Courtois.'

'I reared those animals.'

The soft murmur in response, words inaudible, fails to stop him from continuing. 'That,' he says clearly, his tone bitterly sardonic, 'is how I am "helping" to fight this war, Pontellier!'

'Look, you're helping *us*. Mireille. She mightn't have survived without you, without your parcels.'

'You're my only friend,' he says simply, by way of explanation, then pauses as if defeated. 'How is she faring?'

'Oh,' he sighs, 'so so. She's still a little . . . a little difficult at times but . . . it's nothing I'm not used to by now. I don't know, she barely acknowledges the world beyond her windowsill – comprehends nothing of the current situation. Nor does she, I believe, even care.'

'Perhaps it's better that way. You don't want a recurrence.'

'True.'

'I should volunteer, shouldn't I? At least it would give me something to do.'

'The same could be said for me, my friend. I've no business to speak of at present.'

'It's really that bad?'

'Who has the money for a glass eye in times such as these?'

'I'm sorry.'

'This siege can't last for ever. Something will have to give before too long.'

In the hallway, while the two men have been speaking, Madame Pontellier has let the weight of her body slide slowly downwards against the wall. She is sitting now upon the floor, her legs pulled up before her. Her hands are clasped around her ankles. She can feel the cold of the tiles through her dress. The two men sitting at the desk in the shop space are out of her view. Their conversation barely distracts her, only the sound is what interests her, the shape of it in the dark hallway.

16th of December 1870

In the small hours of an austere December morning, the sky still dense with darkness, Pontellier is jolted from fretful dreams by the sound of screaming. His heart is launched instantly into a galloping frenzy which pounds heavy in his eardrums, vying with the noise that had awoken him. On opening, his eyes see nothing, too recently shielded by sleep are they. They stumble in their attempt to give shape to the sound.

It is the line of her shoulders, distinct beneath the white calico of her nightdress, that comes first into view. The curve of her back and shadowed periphery of her head appearing next, dreamily, like watching the pale torso of a swimmer surface in a dark pool.

He cannot see the black oval of her mouth, nor how it flattens itself each time she pauses to gulp in more breath, her body shuddering with the effort before relaxing itself again into the maintaining of the scream. Her whole consciousness is entirely focused upon the sound, obsessed by it. Its clarity is mesmerising; visible against the night. She can *see* the sound. It is like staring at a bright sun in the sky. That same dazzling funnelled intensity.

At the lace-like edges of the subconscious, her mind tousles with a recollection.

An autumn afternoon, standing in the high-walled garden of her childhood home. She cannot be more than five years old – a sturdy dark-haired child still in short skirts. She isn't alone, but with her parents and a number of others, though she's not quite sure who. They are assembled on the grass, chattering, exuding a nervous excitement. A voice above her says, 'Listen,

Mireille, even the birds have stopped their singing. You hear?'
She nods, straining her ears to listen to the silence beyond
them. The air is close as if waiting for a thunderstorm. 'Help
her with the spectacles so she can have a look,' says another
voice, and someone fumbles to catch the arms of a pair of
wire-rimmed glasses about her ears. The lenses are so dark an
indigo as to be almost black. The wire rests heavy on the
bridge of her nose. 'Up there, look at the sun,' they say, guid-
ing her gaze. And, where a moment before she remembered
the bright haze of the sun, she now sees stencilled into the dark
indigo sky of the spectacles a small white crescent moon. She
grins at this curious trick. The moon is gone again as soon as
they remove the glasses. Only if she squints at the brightness,
then closes her eyes, can she see clearly the little crescent tattooed beneath her eyelids. 'Careful,' says someone, 'if you
stare too long at the sun it will leave you blind.'

Too frightened to look upwards again, she keeps her eyes
downcast, staring at the grass, until that moment when, on
that autumn afternoon of her childhood, the moon's shadow
shifted fractionally in the sky above and the world slipped into
darkness.

When the Wasps Drowned

THAT WAS THE SUMMER THERESE STEPPED ON
the wasps' nest and brought an end to our barefoot wander-
ings, when the sun shone every day and everybody comment-
ed upon it. Old ladies on park benches, fanning themselves
with well-thumbed issues of *Woman's Own*, would sigh, 'Oh,
isn't it hot?' And I, hungry for conversation, would sit tall on
the wooden seat and smile as I agreed, eyes darting to see if
they might say anything more. The heat was all anyone ever
seemed to speak of, and I knew that when the weather
changed we'd still be talking of the same thing, only then we'd
be blowing at our hands and complaining of the cold.

The chemist sold out of after-sun that summer, and
flowerbeds dried up, and people had to queue to get into the
swimming pool. With towels hung over their arms or
squashed into carrier bags, we'd see them waiting along the
wall outside, listening to the shouts echoing on the water within, envious of those who emerged coolly with hair slicked
damp and eyes pinkened by chlorine, carrying bags of crisps
from the vending machine.

It was the first time the garden walls seemed confining,
when finally I was tall enough to peer over their mossy tops

and look across the line of gardens and see sheets, dried out in the heat, listless in the still air, and hear the tinny music of distant transistor radios, and the ache of cars moving slowly in the hot sun, their windows wide as if that might change anything.

That was the summer they dug up Mr Mordecai's garden.

We heard her screams from inside. I was standing at the sink, barefoot on the lino, washing up the breakfast dishes, soaping them lazily as I watched the light play on the bubbles. Tyler was curled under the kitchen table pushing a toy truck back and forth, smiling at the rattle of its metal wheels. Her screaming, the way it broke the day, so shocked me that I dropped a glass, which smashed on the tap and fell into the dishwater below. She was running in circles round the garden, shrieking, a halo of angry wasps blurring her shape, her pigtails dancing.

For the first few moments I just stood, mouth agape, watching her through the grime of the kitchen window, not wanting to go anywhere near Therese or all those wasps. As I ran to the back door, Tyler rose and toddled after me. I remember him laughing as I turned the hose on her – he thought it all a joke. Dripping with water, her sun dress clinging to a polka-dot of red welts, Therese continued to scream into the afternoon. Around her on the grass, wasps lay dark on their backs, legs kicking, wings too sodden to fly.

Mum was out at work all day, leaving us to our own devices. Sometimes I'd take them out, Therese picking at her scabs, Tyler strapped in the buggy. We'd walk down to the park and I'd sit by the swings and watch the boys. They'd stand in a huddle by the public loos, puffing on cigarettes.

Other days we'd just lie in the garden and absorb the heat. I'd fashioned a bikini from a pair of pink knickers and an old vest which I'd cropped just below my nipples. I had a pair of green plastic sunglasses I'd bought at the corner shop and the yellow flipflops Mum now insisted we wear. I'd sunbathe while Therese scoured the grass for wasp corpses. When she found one she'd place it on a paving slab and, using a stone, pound its body to dust. Tyler would squat sagely beside her. I'd watch them idly, lift an arm perhaps to point out another dead wasp lodged between blades of grass.

It was maybe early August when she and Tyler started to dig under the garden wall. Sitting in its shadow, they scratched away with sticks, collecting the dry earth in a plastic bucket. 'Help us, Eveline,' they'd say, 'we're digging to Australia,' but I'd just roll my eyes and turn the page of my magazine. The task would occupy them for a while and then they'd come and loll next to me. Tyler flat out on his stomach, snuffling as the grass tickled his nostrils, Therese plaiting together thin strands of my hair.

So we'd lie and wait for Mum to come home, her uniform sweaty round the edges. Then she'd sit, her legs up on one of the kitchen chairs, complaining how her feet were swollen, watching as we prepared the fish fingers or chicken nuggets.

In that heat, everything seemed an effort. There was a day I remember; I was lying on my side, eyes closed. Therese, finished her digging, was flopped next to me. One plump arm was curled in a damp embrace around my knee. She was breathing hotly against my hip. I opened my eyes in a slow squint against the sun. Therese's other arm was flung out above her head.

It was the glint that caught my eye. I only saw it as she jerked her hand at the buzz of a fly. Wedged on her thumb was a thin gold ring, studded with small diamonds. There was dirt lodged between the stones, but still they caught the sunlight and glimmered. At first I didn't react. I just lay there, watching.

'Therese,' I said finally, 'where'd you get that ring?'

'Found it,' she sighed.

I heaved myself up by one elbow and took her hand in mine to look more closely at the small piece of jewellery. 'Where?' I asked.

Therese yawned before rolling onto one side and up. She walked me to the hole they'd been digging. It was deep and long now, tunnelling under our wall and into Mr Mordecai's garden. We knelt down and peered into its depths. It was too dark to see much. Therese took my hand and guided it into the hole. Straight away I knew what it was I could feel, but I told Therese to run in and find the torch. She came back a moment later and we angled the light. At the end of the tunnel, a pale hand reached towards us.

We said nothing as we looked. The skin was mauve in places, the fingernails chipped and clogged with soil. Suddenly the day around us seemed unbearably quiet, as if everything was holding its breath.

'Therese,' I said eventually, 'I think we'd better fill up the hole.'

We collected the plastic bucket and shunted the piles of earth back where they came from, patting the ground flat with our hands.

Leaning across to her, I took the ring from Therese's thumb and slipped it onto my right index finger. She didn't protest.

And so the digging stopped. We ignored the bald patch of earth by the fence, the mark of the aborted Australia project. The ring I cleaned with an old toothbrush and wore sometimes, but only ever while Mum was at work.

The long days continued to melt into one another. Mum would put us to bed and it would still be light outside. Beyond the curtained windows the world continued and we could hear it all, ever clearer than winter nights when it was dark. Tyler and Therese were too hot and tired to feel they might be missing anything but I would lie awake under the sheets, listening to the street and the muffle of Mum's radio downstairs.

One night Therese woke crying from a bad dream. She padded through to Mum's room and I could hear them across the landing, Mum's voice comforting and sleepy, Therese's diluted by her tears, 'and I was watering the garden, Mum, with a blue watering can, and it started to grow . . .'

'Sleep now, my love, shhh.' I wanted Mum's gentle shush in my own ear. When I closed my eyes I could see Therese's dream, the arm growing up through the soil.

The holidays began finally to peter to a close. The days were still stifled by the heat and, at a loss as to how we might fill them, we'd even begun to miss going to school. Very occasionally, Mum would leave sweet money. Then we'd buy Smarties, lick the shells of the red ones, and rub swathes of scarlet food colouring across our lips. That's what we were doing when we heard the doorbell ring. I flipflopped through the cool of the house to open the front door. A man and a woman stood on the step.

'Is Mum or Dad in, love?' As she asked the question, he peered over our shoulders into the hallway.

I blinked up at them through my sunglasses. Therese and Tyler were both clinging to my bare legs, Tyler fingering the elastic of my bikini bottom. Pouting Smartie-red lips, I told them Mum was at work, wouldn't be home until six. I held my right hand behind my back.

The woman bent towards us and smiled. I tried to stand taller. 'Maybe you can help us then. We're from the police; we just want to ask a couple of questions.' She held out a photograph of a late-teenage girl. A holiday pic. The girl was sun-browned, smiling at something beyond the camera lens. 'Do you think you might have seen this girl?'

We all looked, then shook our heads.

'Are you sure?' She held the photo closer. 'You wouldn't have seen her on the street or anything?'

We all shook our heads again. The man loosened his collar, wiped a trickle of perspiration from his forehead. He caught my glance and smiled. I didn't smile back.

'Well, that's all, then,' said the woman, lowering the picture to her side. 'You've been very helpful, thank you.' She stretched out a hand to ruffle Tyler's curls. He pressed closer against my leg.

I shut the door and we waited a while, heard them walking down our garden path and unlatching Mr Mordecai's gate next door. My fingers, fiddling unconscious, played with the ring for a moment as we stood together in the dark hallway. None of us said a thing. Taking Therese and Tyler by the hand, I turned, and we stepped back out into the sunlight of the garden.

Folks Like Us

I WOULDN'VE PUT MYSELF A MAN WHO BELIEVED in destiny or nothin, not at that time, guess I was more of a free spirit, if you know what I mean, but it was the damnedest thing, 'cause I knew straight away when I saw her that she was the one, standin there like she was with the afternoon light behind her, the door bell still jinglin. She was real tiny, her taffy-colored hair kinked all over her head like a baby's, and dressed purdy nice too, like you could tell it mattered to her, even with times bein as they were, you know, and I just walked on over and I guess tole her my name or somethin and she said, *Oh yeah?* Real self-assured she sounded at first, but as her eyes met mine it was like you could see right on through to the girl in her for a second and she had to look down to the floorboards. Her red mouth was tryin to rein in a smile and this pink started climbin up above the blue of her neckerchief and, would you know it, but for a minute there she almost had me pinkin like a beet too, which was crazy, you know, 'cause I was a man who'd traveled four states and seen a lot of things, but then she looked up, still wrestlin in that smile, and said, *Well hi, my name's Bonnie*, and I just thought she was 'bout the most purdy thing I'd ever seen and I do believe I tole her so and that pink blush was climbin up her face as fast as you'd know it, *Well thank you, sir*, was all she said, and then she walked on over to the counter and made her purchases, I don't rightly remember what, and walked on out the store, that smile finally breakin loose, and I followed her with my eyes, goin 'cross the street, the door bell in the store still janglin, and the fella at the counter started to laugh, seein me standin there all gapin like a guppy and he gave me a look that said, *I think you done taken a shine to that girl*, and I gave him a look right back sayin, *Mister, you could be right*, and then I saw her take a corner and be gone, and I turned to the fella and tole him, *I'll be havin me a packet of your finest tobacco, if you please.*

Weren't a while fore I discovered me she worked at waitressin in a diner, servin up bowls of soup and piss-poor coffee to hungry fellas with tattoos who'd slap her rear end and call out to her as she came past with her arms tied up holdin a tray of dishes. Well it weren't exactly the type of establishment I'd usually frequent, but I'd take me a seat at a corner table and when my mug emptied she'd come on over and give me a refill, not that I was wantin it, that coffee bein so bad, but it gave me the opportunity to ask her a word or two. She could say some awful funny things, and that sure surprised me, I'll tell you, what with her seemin that bashful an all when I'd first encountered her. Fact one time I done asked her about that occasion and she said, *Aw, that's just a show I put on to make the boys fall for me*, then she laughed and I guess I looked pretty dumb 'cause she up and said, *Well, it worked, didn it?* And before I had a chance to think 'bout the meanin of what she said she'd turned right around and slipped back behind the counter, and you know, I weren't sure what to believe but I soon got to thinkin I'd never afore met a gal like this one.

Came a time though when it weren't lookin so favorable for me to be hangin around Dallas no more, but fool that I am I didn want to skip town without sayin goodbye, so I hung

82

around nearabouts her diner until she finished her shift and caught her on her way out the rear door. *Jeepers*, that girl hollered, *you scared the livin daylights outta me. Keep it down*, I hushed her quickly, not wantin to draw 'tention to ourselves, and tole her that a fella was only wonderin if he could walk her home, so she lifted her eyes at me, play-actin as if she might say no, then shrugged her shoulders and said she guessed she wouldn object. But after that I didn know what to say, and we walked along uncomf'tably in silence for a full block, until finally I done asked her how she liked her job, and she shook her head as if to say, *After all that time, that's the best question he can come up with? Job ain't so bad*, was what she replied, but you could tell it in her voice she found it kinda tiresome, *Folk out of work as they are, I can't be complainin*, and I had to agree with her there, but then I up and come out with somethin I weren't predictin at all, I said in that case I s'posed she probably wouldn consider the notion of takin a trip with me. She gave me a suspicious kinda smile, *And where would this trip be goin?* she said, and I sort of laughed and said I didn rightly know, but I'd sure as hell like to take a trip with her, and then I corrected myself 'cause I remembered you ain't s'posed to say *hell* in front of a lady, and I said maybe Missouri would be a good place to take a trip to, and at that she started laughin her head off, stoppin there right on the sidewalk because she couldn walk for laughin, *Missouri? And what would I tell my momma and the girls at work?* and I tole her I was sure we could come up with somethin so they'd be obligin, but the thing of it was we'd have to be leavin that same night, and now she really did look at me like I was crazy, but then she went quiet and said, *Okay then.*

So we planned on meetin up later that evenin, and I tole her to pack a bag an all, and when I pulled in at her drive she must've been watchin for me 'cause she came straight out from around back. It kinda angered me at the time and I guess it shouldn've, but she took her own sweet time walkin down that path, real slow she went, and I was sittin in the car feelin butterflies skeetin about in my belly, and so I just said *Hi* when she got in the front seat and she just said *Hi,* and for a moment it was like we was strangers again, and I pulled away real fast and started drivin down the road. I was drivin a Ford V-8 sedan at the time, which I knew would impress her with its speed, for those cars always have been my partic'lar favorite, though I'm prepared to settle for a coupé if there ain't no V-8 sedans available, but anyways, after a while I says to her, *Well, did you say anythin to your momma?* and she just said, *no,* she thought as how she'd just send a picture postcard or somethin from the next town, and I flicked my eyes off the road for a second 'cause I thought she might be cryin just a little, but in the light of the streetlamps I could see her cheeks were dry, but I guess she knew even then that there weren't gonna be no postcards.

It was only later, when we'd stopped for a bite to eat, that she asked me what it was I did. I knew the question would be comin up of course, but I hadn't quite reckoned yet at what I'd tell her, so I jus sat there watchin her, me chewin my food around in my mouth, and she kept up watchin me, and neither she or me said nothin for a short while, and it did cross my mind to tell her a falsehood, but in the end I came out with it and tole her as how I'd just been doin a stint in the state penitentiary, held up for armed robbery, and she didn move a muscle or say a thing and I guessed she was wonderin what in hell she was doin sittin here in a highway diner a good three hours from her hometown with a guy she hardly knew who happened to be in possession of not much more than a criminal record, but then you know what that girl gone done and said? – she says to me, *Guess it beats waitressin, huh?*

We stopped outside a motel and went on in to reception, the whole parlor was stinkin with cigar smoke and there behind the desk was a creaky ole fella chewin on the sog-end of a cigar, well he brightened up some when he saw how purdy

Bonnie was, and asked how he could help us, and I said we'd be havin us a room, if he pleased, and then I looked to Bonnie who'd stepped away to stare at some picture or other, and added, as an afterthought, *Twin beds please, mister, for me and my wife.* The ole fella nodded and started runnin his fingers across a row of keys hangin on the wall behind him, then handed one over and had us sign our names in a book. Well our room weren't nothin special, but I guess it was the first time Bonnie had stayed in a hotel and she looked all around it and ran the faucets just to try them, and turned on the light between the beds, and felt the covers between her fingers, and leafed through the bible that was parked on the table, and then sat down facin me on the other bed, *So*, was what she said, *I heard you tell that ole fella I was your wife.* There was a sly smile on her face so I couldn discern if she were angry with me or not, but so as she would understand she could count on me to be a respectable fella, I tole her I'd leave her for a bit so she could change in private an all. I stepped out onto the porch to have a cigarette and when I came back in later the room was dark but for that tiny light. She'd folded her clothes up neat and laid them on her bag, and she was all tucked up in the far bed, the blanket pulled right up to her chin, her hair spread out on the pillow. Suddenly I felt kinda strange just standin there, the cigarette smoke and the night still clingin to the silk of my shirt, her in bed like some little child and me her poppa, and she weren't sayin nothin, and tell you the truth, the quiet started makin me uncomf'table so I done asked her if everythin was okay, and she said, *Yeah, it's all fine*, and I said that was good, then I just stood there in the dark a bit longer, and we both of us kept quiet till I said, *So you gonna go to sleep or somethin?* and she said, *Guess so*, but still she kept up lyin there in that bright circle of lamplight with her eyes wide open, not makin no move to turn out the light, and I stood there a bit longer and sort of looked around me until finally I just said it, *So ain't you gonna turn your eyes away or somethin so I can get to bed?* – Well, at that she shifted under the covers quick smart so as her back was to me, and I slipped off my clothes fast as I could, not foldin them neatly or nothin, jumped under the sheets of that other bed and switched out the light, we lay there silent in the dark for a bit and then I said, *Goodnight*, and a small voice came across in reply, sayin, *G'night, Clyde*.

She was a strange girl, that much I'll say for her, almost like whatever it was had made her couldn make up its mind. Sure she could be crackly and sharp as a pine needle, and she had a mouth on her dirtier'n some of 'em I heard in the State Pen, but to start off there was more times as she'd go and show herself unknowin and eager as a li'l kid, startin out in a life they didn understand but wanted a part of. When all them different sides was rolled together what came out was Bonnie, and as I done said, she may not have turned out the gal I'd first thought she was, but I didn care, cause I done liked her all the more each day, and that's a fact. Boy, she was somethin, like how she could put on a show, you know, fake actin and dancin about and pretendin like she was some goddamn fat-bellied opera singer, makin me laugh real hard, I'm tellin you. Hell, that girl had a comeback for every wisecrack I could come out with, oh yeah she was real bright, she sure weren't never short of spirit, fact she reminded me of one of them fairground balloons, like she was filled with gas and could have lifted up into the sky any moment, only, and this was the one thing that bothered me sometimes, it felt to me like somehow I was tied on to her and holdin her down on the ground, and one night I done tole her that thought and she just looked at me and tole me not to be dumb, I remember her sayin it, *Don't be dumb, Clyde Barrow*, she said, *for if that's the case, don't you see that it's you that's set me flyin?*

And I like to think she was right. She'd seen a time of it and I wasn't the first free spirit with a record she'd found herself tied up with. It was a June day I'm thinkin, real early on after we'd started drivin, and the sun was hot as a potato, and we got ourselves a little engine trouble just outside Fayetteville, so I pulled off my shirt and set to work under the hood. Well that gal climbed out after a while and said as how she did surely believe it was just too hot to breathe. I was too busy to answer her, so she kept up, *It's so damn hot I think I'm surely gonna melt; it's so damn hot I think my eyes are gonna roll right outta my head; it's so goddamn hot I think my hair's gonna frazzle like as it's spent too long under the curlin irons*, I just kept up my tinkerin, and then she swings her head under the hood, looks me over real slow as I'm doing my work, and says, *So who's Gladys?* Well, I didn say nothin for a moment cause I guessed she'd as likely be pretty mad, specially when she up and saw that I'd got *Anne* tattooed on the other arm. Finally I just says, *Gladys was a gal I once thought might mean somethin but didn*, and she said, *Oh yeah?* and I said, *Yeah, same with the Anne who got herself writ on my other side*, and when I looked up then I saw she was smilin, and that surprised me, so I done asked her about it, and she didn say nothin, just stepped back from the car and lifted up her skirt hem, and there, blue above her stockin top in wavy cursive was *Roy*, and that girl started laughin and said, *Sure as he means nothin too, and he's stuck in the State Pen for first-degree murder*, and so that was how I learned about her husband.

Each day we'd drive, didn know where we was goin, didn care. I'm recallin a certain day on the road when she'd been gettin antsy and had clambered on over into the back seat, and lay there for a while, her bare feet stickin out the window into the sunlight, then she sat up and leant her arms over the seat and sighed real long as she watched the road go by. Finally, she takes another sigh and says to me, *I'm gonna be a poet, Clyde*, she said it in a real clear voice but first off I just thought she was kiddin around, so I gone and come out with some wisecrack like, *Yeah, and I'm gonna be the President of the United States*. Now this made her kinda mad, which surprised me an all, 'cause she crossed her arms and slid right away across the seat and her face went black as a darn thunder cloud, *You just see*, she scolded me, *I've known it since I was a little girl in short socks. I'm gonna be a poet.*

So that was some surprise but it was fine with me, I'd never paid much 'tention in school myself, but as I've tole you, Bonnie was real smart and I guess it could be said she had a way with words, so next time we stopped at a store I left her out front and went on in on my own. It was a store stuck out on the road, one of those funny little places that sell everythin and nothin if you know what I mean, so it didn come as no surprise that there weren't no one in there but myself and the ole cowboy behind the cash register, one of them ole tobacco spitters, you know, his boots up on the desk, pickin away at a ukulele. Well, it pleased me to hear that and I tole him so, tole him 'bout the time we bought the ukulele and didn know how to tune it nor had the money to find out for ourselves – that ole cowboy still playin away while I talked – and how I had the bright idea of orderin out a few penny tubs of ice cream knowin that when the nigger boy came to deliver he'd sure be able to tune up the instrument and show us all how to play it. Well, the ole fella behind the desk laughed at that and I laughed with him, and then he done asked me what it was I'd be wantin, so I tole him I'd like a school book, somethin with lines on the pages for writin out poems, and a couple of pencils, and he picked out those and set them out on the desk, then I had him cut me a few slices of baloney and a chunka cheese – in all it didn come to no more'n a few dimes, but when he up and asked for the money I took out my li'l .32 Colt, as was my custom, and said I'd be preferrin it if he could hand over whatever he might have in the register. Well, his look turned black and ornery when he realized what was up but there weren't nothin that ole cowboy could do but open up the register and hand over the cash; I stuffed it in my pocket, took my purchases under my arm, and started up edgin back out the store, keepin my Colt pointed in his direction all the time. Well, he just stood there, stiff as a poker behind the glass of the meats counter, and all was quiet but for the buzzin of a coupla flies hummin over the cold cuts. It coulda ended like that, fact a part of me wishes it had, wishes I'd remembered first up what else it was I'd been wantin, but you can't change events and the fact was I'd forgotten up till then so instead I just stepped a pace forward and tole him, *I'm awful sorry, but I just remembered I'll also be needin me a pencil sharp'ner, could you be obligin?* The ole fella jus nodded without sayin a word, turned his back to me and started lookin about behind him, and that's when I saw that his hand was inchin toward the meat cleaver. I do regret it had to be that way, 'cause tell you the truth I'd been rather fond of the fella afore that, but it surely made me lose my appetite for the baloney to see him crumple behind his counter that way, him bein white haired an all, and how fast those darn flies buzzed over to him, and I turned on my heel and walked out the store. Outside Bonnie was pokin her head out the front window, and when she saw my Colt still smoking she hollered at me, *God damn you, Clyde Barrow, can't you just go in a store like a normal person for once?* Well, I weren't in no mood for that kinda talk, so I just fired up the sedan and threw the notebook and pencils in her lap, sayin, *These is for your poems. I couldn get you no sharp'ner.*

Hell now those was happy days though, even if we knew they couldn last forever. Sure we spent a lot of time in the car, listenin to the radio, Fred Waring Orchestra or somethin of the like, Bonnie scribblin in her books or flickin through one of those detective magazines she was so fond of. Sure it was a long time but I tell you we got to lovin the hum of the wheels below us and the world goin by, felt we was goin somewhere, which is more than can be said for most folk, those as who we'd see sittin out on their porches as we drove through the towns, no work to distract them from the passin of time. Sure I know that's all life is, just a long road stretchin up afore you, and you knowin sure as hell there's gonna be a dead end comin up ahead sooner or later, but damn it felt good to be hitched to someone who had ambition, Bonnie knew where she was goin and she was takin me with her. Each time she'd finish up a poem she'd write it out in her best hand and we'd get hold of a coupla stamps and send them out to the papers. I'm not sayin it weren't hard at first, gettin hold of the rags a few days later and flickin through, her eyebrows crinkling as she ran her eyes across the pages, and sometimes there'd be a mention of the two of us, which could distract for a moment, but then she'd continue on until she hit the back page and always it was the same, the paper fallin loose from her grip and her kickin at the dash and sayin to me, *Damn editors.*

Time came soon enough when it weren't so sensible to be checkin ourselves into motels an all, for there were plenty out there who would've been mighty pleased to pick up the bounty on my head. Sometimes there'd be folks I'd know who'd put us up for a night or two, rest of the time we'd just turn off the road when it started gettin dark and roll back the seats in the car or just set down blankets on the grass, sleep in all our clothes and stuff just in case we might need to make a hasty exit. There was one morning we'd woke up and the air was warm and a light breeze was shufflin through the tree tops. We was lyin under a sycamore stuck next to a dirt track, and Bonnie goes and asks me, *What will we do when we is old, Clyde?* I was chewin on a stalk of corn watchin the sky, *Guess we'll have made our way back home to Texas, and each day I'll wake up and cook you some eggs, and we'll live in the biggest house in the state, and there'll be a boy'll come and shine our shoes each day and a girl as'll clean the house, so as you can spend your hours sittin out on the porch writin in your books.* Bonnie shifted over onto her back to smile at me, *You know, Clyde, I think every goddamn day I'll wear diamonds and silk stockins, even if I'm just walkin down to the store or somethin, and we'll find you a nice hat, the nicest hat in Texas.* I sure liked the sounda that hat. *How many kids'll we have, you think?* I asks her. *Eight, maybe nine, hey? That's a good number, ain't it?* and 'fore I could say, *Surely, honey,* she's kissin at my left ear and gigglin to think on it.

What happened next all went so fast I didn know what was going on at first. 'Fore I knew it, Bonnie's scrambled up and grabbed at my Colt which we always have close by us when we sleep, and a shot rings out, so damn loud it feels like the sky might crack up, and there was a fallin and a crash and then there was this goddamn fella in a sheriff's uniform lyin just a nickel's width from Bonnie's toe. For a second there she just stood quiet and watched that fella lyin on the dirt. He was crumpled over himself, left leg bent back crooked, right arm reachin out almost to Bonnie's foot, a pistol ridgin the dirt where it'd skidded from his hand, big face slammed up against the gravel, fat lips gookin out like a baby's might when sucklin, eyes still as marbles. And Bonnie just stood there quiet, her face pinched in like a doughball. She didn say nothin. I'd sat up and I could feel the sun hot on my neck and I could feel a trickle of sweat travelin down 'tween my shoulder blades, real slow like, ticklin plenty, but still I didn curve back my arm to wipe it away. Then she done turns to me and out slips them thoughts that is skeetin through her mind, *Clyde . . . Clyde . . . what you think? Maybe he's not dead, Clyde. You know it, maybe he's just fakin. Whyn't you get over there and see if he's breathin or somethin?* But I didn move nor say nothin and already her eyes is back on that fella and she's watchin how his blood is spreadin out quick and dark upon the ground, just like a vehicle losin gasoline. *What you think, Clyde?* and she lifts her shoe and just sways it at his hand lyin there like a chunka dog meat, and that hand done turns over so its palm is lyin up to us, fingers still curled over, and up above us we can hear birds in the sky, and still I don't wipe at that trickle of sweat, and not liftin her eyes from the fella Bonnie says to me, *He was just comin for us with his pistol,* and then quiet but almost like she's tryin to hold back laughin or somethin else,

Guess I done it then, huh? Still I don't say nothin, and then, like one of them tall scrawny birds you see in the marshlands, she stretches out her toe and just lowers it slow into the blood, and starts up writin somethin in the dirt. B . . . O . . . she has to stretch back like dippin a pen in ink, then an N, and she's just startin up on another of them when I say, *Bonnie . . .* and then again a bit louder, *Bonnie*, and she whirls around like one of them child's toys, you know, that you pull the string out of and it goes spinnin 'cross the floorboards, *Well hell, Clyde.*

Bonnie sat shotgun that day as we drove, arms crossed in front of her, face ornery as hell, starin silent out the window. Finally, she looks down at her feet and bends up her left knee so as her foot is on the seat, she spends a while examinin her shoe, spittin upon her finger and scrubbin some at the dark patch that has spread across the satin of the toe, then she says out loud, *These shoes is ruined*, and she yanks that shoe off her foot and hurls it out the window – I can see it bouncin along the highway in the driver's mirror – next she throws out the other one for good measure, then she sets up again, arms crossed. 'Bout twenty minutes more down the road, not one word been said by neither of us, her just starin, her eyebrows hangin low above her eyes, she suddenly goes, *Oh Clyde, I feel sick, I feel sick as a dog, Clyde. Stop the car, will ya? Oh Lord, I feels sick.* So I pulls up on the side and she jumps out and starts hurlin up her guts all over the dirt, and finally when it's all over and I got her cleaned up, she curls up on the front seat with her head restin in my lap as I drive, *Guess it was somethin I ate last night, don't you think, Clyde?* and I just dropped my hand to stroke her hair and said, *Sure it is, honey, just somethin bad you ate last night.*

She were sort of quiet and cranky the next few days and I didn pester her much about it, just left her scribblin in her notebooks more than ever. *You writin poems?* I'd ask her, and she'd just say, *Uh huh*, and she'd be chewin on her pencil and would be too stuck in them books to even look up. So I'd just fix my eyes on the road and keep drivin, and sometimes there'd come someone followin up behind us but I'd just drive a little faster and most times we could shake 'em off, and other days the road would be long and quiet and maybe I'd whistle along to somethin on the radio if that didn bother her, or maybe I'd just say, *I knows you'll be famous one day with them poems*, and she'd just say, *Yeah sure, Clyde*, but she'd say it without even lookin up, almost like she weren't really listenin, you know, so I'd go on, *Sure you'll be famous and we'll go back to Texas and get me that hat and bring up them nine babies*, and all of a sudden she turns to me and just stares for a little while and then she done says, *Clyde, how the hell you think we're gonna have nine babies? Where we gonna keep 'em? In the back of the goddamn car?*

But sure as hell, turned out it was me that was right, 'cause I tole her they'd sit up and take notice one day. We'd both of us been feelin for a while that we'd give near anythin for a night or two in a real bed, and Bonnie, she had an achin for a plate of home-cooked red beans, so we swung about and headed on down to Joplin, Missouri, knowin as how Joplin had a reputation for being a pretty safe kinda place if you know what I mean. I set myself up as a Mr. W. J. Callahan, a visitin civil engineer from Minnesota, and got myself an apartment on the corner of 34th Street. We just laid out for a coupla days, ate them beans till we felt like we'd bust, and exercised our legs by strollin 'bout the livin room. It was a Sunday mornin, a real bright day but we had the curtains closed, nat'rally, and I was stretched out under the sheets makin the most of that king-size mattress and when I weren't dozin I'd been watchin Bonnie through the doorway sittin at the table in her negligee and house slippers writin out one of her poems. By that point though she was done doin with that and had pushed it away to lay out a hand of solitaire. Next thing she glanced out through a slit between the curtains then jumped right outta her seat

93

sayin, *Hell, honey, it's the laws!* Sure didn take us long to get outta that place, and I can tell you there were a few bullets flyin, but once again our lucky stars were shinin above us and we was okay, only when the hoo-haw had calmed down and we was back out on the road Bonnie started cursin her head off, *Damn it*, she was sayin, her fists punchin away at the dash, *Goddamn and hell, I forgot my poem*, and then, *We've gotta go back for it, we've gotta*. Took a while to quieten her down and make her see sense, there weren't no way we could go back to Joplin, place would be crawlin by that time, but we was both pretty sad 'cause she'd showed me that poem and I thought it was 'bout the best thing she'd ever done and I'd tole her so and it sure was a shame that it should be forgotten. But that weren't the end of it, for as you'll be knowin, the Lord works in mysterious ways, 'cause next day I got me a newspaper and guess what should be on the front page? Sure that's right, and boy was Bonnie pleased. I tell you it was a swell day, just to see her words printed up, and right next to that poem a picture of the two of us that the police must have found in the apartment, taken in front of the Ford, Bonnie posin with a shotgun, and right below that the news, which was how we found out 'bout the two law officers who'd passed away. So Bonnie ups and tells me to get drivin afore we go get ourselves caught, and then she sits up straight on that front seat and holds out the newspaper afore her and in a real clear voice reads that poem out loud, and the wind was comin through the windows and blowin her hair all about and carryin her words back out into the world, and hell I thought my heart would bust.

The Story of Bonnie and Clyde

You've read the story of Jesse James –
Of how he lived and died;
If you're still in need
Of something to read,
Here's the story of Bonnie and Clyde.

Now Bonnie and Clyde are the Barrow gang,
I'm sure you all have read
How they rob and steal
And those who squeal
Are usually found dying or dead.

There's lots of untruths to these write-ups;
They're not so ruthless as that;
Their nature is raw;
They hate all the law –
The stool pigeons, spotters, and rats.

They call them cold-blooded killers;
They say they are heartless and mean;
But I say this with pride,
That I once knew Clyde
When he was honest and upright and clean.

But the laws fooled around,
Kept taking him down
And locking him up in a cell,
Till he said to me,
'I'll never be free,
So I'll meet a few of them in hell.'

The road was so dimly lighted;
There were no highway signs to guide;
But they made up their minds
If all roads were blind,
They wouldn't give up till they died.

The road gets dimmer and dimmer;
Sometimes you can hardly see;
But it's fight, man to man,
And do all you can,
For they know they can never be free.

From heart-break some people have suffered;
From weariness some people have died;
But take it all in all,
Our troubles are small
Till we get like Bonnie and Clyde.

[. . .]

From Irving to West Dallas viaduct
Is known as the Great Divide,
Where the women are kin,
And the men are men,
And they won't stool on Bonnie and Clyde.

If they try to act like citizens
And rent them a nice little flat,
About the third night
They're invited to fight
By a sub-gun's rat-tat-tat.

They don't think they're too tough or desperate,
They know that the law always wins;
They've been shot at before,
But they do not ignore
That death is the wages of sin.

Some day they'll go down together;
And they'll bury them side by side;
To few it'll be grief –
To the law a relief –
But it's death for Bonnie and Clyde.

Bonnie Parker (1934)

Safe

THEY STARTED TO DISAPPEAR IN FEBRUARY.
The first in a shopping centre in Leeds, right beneath the watch
of a security camera. One moment there was a baby, strapped
in its carriage as the mother leant to look in the window of a
shop selling sports shoes; the next moment, gone.

Just like that. As if someone had spliced the camera film.

Standing alone, the case was unexplained, yet still unextra-
ordinary. It was only after a pattern started to emerge – a
fourth baby disappearing without trace – that the Leeds
CCTV footage made the national news.

After that, there were two more in one week. One from a
park in Edinburgh, another from a hospital ward in Hull.
Then two from private homes which reported all doors and
windows locked. And then came the case in Hampshire with
the moving car.

The Police Commissioner made a statement. He stood for
the cameras before the revolving blue sign of New Scotland
Yard and instructed the public not to panic. 'Distressing as
these incidents are,' he reasoned, his voice so reassuring, 'our
best teams of investigators are working round the clock to find
a rational explanation. I am confident we will be returning

these infants safely to their parents in no time at all.'

But the very next night news reports were covering another case, a thirty-something couple from north London whose three-month-old had vanished from her sleepcot.

'Another one?' asked Lella from the doorway.

'Yeah.'

She stood there, on her way up to the bathroom, and instinctively lowered her head to kiss her own baby's crown. Above the milken smell of skin, she paused, her eyes fixed on the couple on the television screen.

'These ones, they look like people like us,' she said.

He made no response.

'It's weird though, isn't it? Makes it seem more . . . kind of more real, you know what I mean?'

''Cause you can't imagine people like them doing their own baby in?'

'I didn't say that.' Her eyes pulled from the television screen. 'That's horrible to even think something like that.'

'It's probably what's happening.'

'You don't know anything.' She turned upstairs to run a bath for the baby.

'Lella,' she heard him cry after her, 'I didn't mean . . . Lel – .'

Locking the door behind her, Lella turned on both the taps.

While she was cleaning the kitchen counter the following morning, her J Cloth swept up three small, blackened scraps, like charred grains of rice. She stopped, and lifted one between her rubber-gloved fingers to study it.

Mouse droppings, was the realisation that came suddenly. Mice. She threw a quick glance about the kitchen, as if she might locate the culprit immediately. But of course there was only herself and the baby, sleeping contentedly in the baby seat placed in the middle of the room. Lella swept the other two scraps into her hand and disposed of them in the bin, then sprayed the whole countertop again with cleaning fluid and wiped it down, wondering if they sold mousetraps in Sainsbury's.

In the following week, three more babies went missing. The police urged new parents to be vigilant. When she was out now, Lella couldn't help noticing the concerned looks people would give her as she passed with the pushchair.

'It's okay,' she wanted to smile back at them, 'I'm keeping her safe.'

But the more they replayed on television the CCTV footage of that first Leeds baby that had gone missing, the one that appeared to just vanish from its carriage as the young mother paused to look in a shop window, the more Lella felt uncomfortable each time she laid the baby in the ergonomic all-terrain carriage they'd purchased at such great expense. It made her nervous to have the baby out of her view as she pushed.

She wasn't the only one, she realised, after she had to try three baby shops before she could find one that hadn't sold out of baby slings.

'Keep 'em close to you this way,' said the shop assistant as she swiped Lella's credit card. 'Can't be too safe right now, can you?'

On the radio that afternoon there was a discussion about the disappearances that Lella was listening to as she fed the baby. Or half-listening, anyway. She kept dropping off, then she'd open her eyes again and once more catch the thread of the discussion, cradling the baby's head with her palm. 'You're hungry today, little girl,' Lella smiled, sleepy from broken nights. Her breasts felt tender. A psychologist was talking about the impact current events were having on the national psyche. The baby made a snuffling sound and clasped her hand around one of Lella's fingers. It was one of the first spring days, and the window was open. Not too wide, because Lella was worried about the baby catching a chill from the draught, but it felt good to let fresh air into the room after the winter months.

'People need to feel safe,' the psychologist was saying, 'they need to feel they can protect,' and that was when Lella heard the noise. A muffled shuffling and scratching. She cocked her head and listened. It was very faint, but she was sure she could hear something. Reaching over, she turned off the radio, still listening. A sound like crumpled newspaper being rustled together, and then a panicky gnawing, coming from the wall behind her, low down. Gently she drew the baby from her breast, laid her on the sofa cushion beside her, and snapped back her bra. The baby started to cry. 'Shh,' hushed Lella, her ear still listening for that new sound. She went behind the sofa and lowered herself on her knees beside the wall. The sound was louder here; scritchy and persistent. Out of her sight, the baby let out another small wail. 'Shh,' said Lella again, as she rested her ear against the wall.

There was definitely something there. Something alive.

Lella was not the kind of woman to be disturbed by rodents. She'd never had a problem with them. But that had been when they were pets, kept in cages that were cleaned regularly, with coloured plastic-tube mazes to climb through and wheels to run in. She was aware now that whatever was making the noise was just inches away from her on the inside of the wall, and the realisation made her body chill suddenly, like everything was shrinking up inside herself. Very slowly, as if she didn't want to disturb whatever it was, she rose again and turned back to the sofa.

Breeze billowed the pale curtain as Lella felt her heart leap and her throat gag with a horrible sick-making shock at what she saw.

There was the baby, lying on the cushion, sucking at its fist in place of Lella's nipple, and right beside it the open window. Anyone could have just reached in.

She told her husband that night. 'I think we have mice.'

'Mice?'

'I've found droppings. And today I heard them in the living-room wall.'

'In the walls? It's more likely rats in London.'

'Please don't say that,' she shuddered, smiling as she poured more wine into his glass.

'Call Rentokil.'

'I did. They said they were experiencing unusually high demand and put me on hold. I waited twenty minutes then gave up. We're missing the news,' she said, glancing at the clock, but as she stood he caught her round the waist and pulled her towards him. For a few moments they embraced.

'You seem a bit better today,' he said.

'Maybe.'

'Let's have an early night,' he whispered against her middle, but as he did he felt her body tense and pull back from him.

'The doctor said wait six weeks, you know that,' she said sharply, and twisted from his embrace.

She worried when the baby was out of her sight now. When she used the bathroom, she took the baby in with her. When she showered, she left the curtain pulled slightly back so she could see her on the bath mat. She took her into bed with them and held her close, shoulders turned to her husband in case he rolled over in his sleep. She would check herself if even just for a moment she turned her back on the baby while in a room with her.

Because that was all it took, a second of inattention. She kept hearing the desperate parents on the news programmes say so, recall how they'd just glanced away for a moment, and when they looked back their babies were gone. Vanished into thin air. That's what they kept saying through their sobs. 'I just got up to switch on the television, and when I looked back he was gone. Vanished into thin air.'

Only the night before she had heard a story like that on the radio. And as she listened, the thought that came to Lella's mind was, 'They couldn't have loved them enough.' She knew it wasn't fair to think this way, but she couldn't banish her belief; 'If they loved them as much as I love my baby, they wouldn't have lost them.'

Eighty-three had now gone missing. A huge number. A number that could no longer be explained away in any rational manner. A number that was perplexing and horrifying the nation. It made no sense. The police still claimed to be making progress, but they hadn't solved a single case. They hadn't found a single baby. Not even the body of a baby. Each further day they remained unfound, the tension in the country was rising.

Lella focused on the faces of the parents in the newspapers, as if in their expressions she might find some clue everyone else was missing. She stared at the baby photos, the rows of missing babies that all started to look alike after a while, and pulled her own baby close against her chest.

'You should stop reading the news,' said her husband, coming into the kitchen to find her poring over an article, the radio playing by her elbow. 'It's not healthy to be obsessing over it so much. Thinking about these things isn't going to help you.'

'What do you know?' she asked him angrily, then regretted it and let him put his arms around her.

She saw it the next day, while she was sitting in the living room feeding the baby. A swift sleek black shape scurrying along the skirting board to disappear into the hallway. So fast that for a second she thought she was hallucinating. She gasped, and the movement shook the baby from her breast. It began to whimper softly, but Lella was still too stunned to react. The creature had been so big. Definitely not a mouse. Bigger than she'd even imagined a rat would be. Yet it must have been a rat, because the image that replayed now in her mind was the movement of the tail curling out of the doorframe. A thick pink tail, like uncooked sausage meat.

This time she remained on the line when they put her on hold. Over forty-five minutes she waited.

'Four weeks at the earliest,' said the woman.

'You can't send someone for four weeks?'

'We've been inundated with calls. There's a nationwide epidemic.'

'I saw in the newspaper, but –'

'I'm really sorry,' said the woman. 'There's nothing I can do. Don't leave any food out. Keep your rubbish bags tied up. We'll send someone as soon as we can.'

'But I have a baby,' said Lella.

The woman paused. 'I'm sorry,' she said.

Lella didn't want to tell her husband, but she was rarely leaving the house these days. She knew the baby was just as vulnerable indoors, but it felt safer this way. Going outside made her nervous. She was jumpy, shied each time somebody came near her.

Exhaustion didn't help. Each night she would lie in the dark, feeling the baby's shallow breath against her neck as she focused blearily on the pattern in the wallpaper or the blinking digits of the clock radio, terrified by the shadows but frightened to close her eyes and lose contact. Instead, her body forced sleep upon her by day, grabbing at it greedily as she sat feeding or reading the paper. Each time she would be jolted from unconsciousness again with a jerk of terror as her mind remembered the baby and panicked wildly for a moment before she realised she was lying safe in her arms.

She didn't want her husband to know she wasn't leaving the house any longer because he'd only worry for her more. She feared he might bring up the idea of a counsellor again. So she was clever about it, and congratulated herself that this was a secret that wasn't so difficult to keep from him. By telephone, she set up an account with the newsagent to have the paper delivered each day. The shopping could be ordered online and delivered to the door. She fabricated visits to friends. It all could be managed. She'd even ordered rat poison online.

Babies were still disappearing. The computerised maps of the country that were displayed on the news each night sprouted more and more cases until they looked like the pincushion her mother used to keep in the sewing chest, each coloured dot marking another missing baby.

She'd taken to wearing the baby in the sling even as she did the housework. It felt safer this way, feeling her close. It was while she was cleaning one of the kitchen cabinets that she found the nest.

The first thing she noticed was tiny scraps of chewed paper, and then a spill of flour and lentils that had escaped from their packages. When she pushed these aside, there at the back of the cupboard she saw a greyish mass of paper and fluff. Like a tiny blanket she might have made as a child for her dolls. She bent lower, careful not to bump the baby, and reached forward with a rubber-gloved hand to slide it towards her.

With a scream, Lella fell back from the cupboard onto her rear. She scooted backwards across the floor, and at her chest the baby's voice rose in a distressed wail. Breathing heavily, Lella leant against the oven door, her legs still sprawled across the kitchen floor, the baby screeching. Her heart was beating in her eardrums. She sat like this for a few minutes, and when she'd eventually calmed a little she crawled forward again on her knees and peered into the cupboard to take another look in the grey nest.

At first she'd thought they were maggots, or worms writhing, but she could see now that what had so surprised her were ten or more rat pups wriggling over and about each other. They were each only about an inch and a half long, a little thinner than her thumb, and perfectly pink. Their flesh hung wrinkled, as if too big for their bodies. Their eyes were still just dark smudges beneath the skin, and their ears not yet distinct from their heads. Their legs were scrabbling, the toes still undefined. Only the tails seemed advanced, almost as thick as their bodies and pink. The small creatures wriggled blindly in the nest, the sight of them turning Lella's stomach.

Breaking her initial paralysis, she grabbed for the tea towel and wrapped it loosely about the nest so she could lift it.

Rising from the floor, she held the bundle gingerly before her, hushing her howling baby as she stepped quickly up the stairs to the bathroom. Before she could allow herself to give it a second thought, she released the towel over the toilet bowl, and watched the tiny pink creatures and the mass of paper and fluff drop. The baby rats were flapping their legs in the water. Horrified, Lella slammed down the lid and pressed the flush. The water gushed, and she stood there, listening until the cistern had fully filled again, then flushed once more before she lifted the toilet lid. The toilet bowl was again empty, the water clear.

Lella dropped suddenly to her knees, and with a violence that frightened her vomited up everything in her stomach. The baby was whimpering, pressed as it was against her thighs and the cold ceramic of the toilet bowl.

Eventually, when Lella could retch no more, she collapsed onto the bathroom floor and curled against the bathtub, sobbing. That was how her husband found her when he returned from work that evening.

The doctor paid them a house call and visited Lella in bed. He took her blood pressure, looked at her tongue, and felt her forehead. 'You must stay in bed,' he advised. 'It's time to take care of yourself now.'

Lella just closed her eyes and wished he would go away.

'Be gentle with her,' she heard him say in a lowered tone beyond the door. 'Her hormones are still unsettled and her body weak. She's been through a lot.' He prescribed some blue pills that would help her sleep, and instructed her husband not to allow her access to the news. 'I'm convinced it's this dreadful business that's brought on the anxiety, seeing all these parents lose their babies.'

Her husband had been given time off work, and he tended to Lella, bringing her cups of tea and boiled eggs that she didn't eat, and the blue pills with cool glasses of water. He watched her put each pill in her mouth and drink from the glass and then, satisfied, he would kiss her on the forehead and leave her to rest. She felt like a little girl. When he was gone, she untucked the pills from beneath her tongue and slipped them over the headboard. She imagined them lined up on the carpet beneath the bed, gathering dust and fluff.

Lella also imagined the babies that she knew must still be disappearing. The ones she wasn't allowed to know about. Not knowing didn't help her fear to wane.

Her own baby she kept in bed with her at all times now, her arms close around her. It was the only way she felt safe. But with so little sleep her body seemed to be losing all its energy, and even lifting herself up against the pillows to feed the child was an effort.

Today, the baby was fractious. Her mouth strained as if she was hungry, but when Lella offered her the nipple she rejected it. Lella sang, and tried to rock her in her arms, but the baby wouldn't quieten. Eventually, Lella decided to try her in the cradle.

It was an effort just to pull back the covers, and when she did, despite the summer's day, Lella felt terribly cold in her thin nightgown. She held the baby against her chest and struggled over to the cradle where she laid her down carefully and tucked a blanket close around her. The baby was still crying, but as Lella rocked she eventually began to hush.

The rhythm of the rocking cradle made Lella's eyelids begin to droop and her head loll. She kept jerking her eyes back open then struggling as desperately they tried again to close. The curtains were drawn against the day, and the only light in the room came from the bedside lamp. The baby was quiet now, lying calm beneath the blanket as the cradle rocked.

Once more Lella's eyes jerked open, and this time she let out a scream. A high, blood-curdling wail of a scream, for there at the foot of the cradle crouched a large grey rat. Its fur was greasy, and it had two long yellow teeth biting beneath a shivering nose. Curled about its side and resting across the baby's feet was the thick pink sausage-meat tail. The rat's black eyes glittered in the light from the bedside lamp, fixed upon Lella.

On the table sat a cold boiled egg in an eggcup, beside four cold soldiers of toast. The butter knife rested on the edge of the plate. Snatching for it, she lifted it high to slash down at the rat, but at that same moment the door flew open.

'A rat!' she screamed, her eyes frantic and wide. 'Help me. There's a rat in the cradle! Look at it! There.'

Her husband grabbed for her wrist and as he clasped it tight the butter knife dropped from her hand. 'No!' she screamed, struggling backwards, her arm still raised above her head, 'Let go of me! I tell you, there's a rat. In the baby's cradle.'

'Lella,' he cried, trying to control her in his arms. 'Calm down. Stop it, stop it now. There's nothing. Look.' He forced her over so she could look. 'You see, *nothing*. You're fantasising, Lella. There's *nothing* there!'

She can't even scream. She can't yell. She can't do anything. Because he's right. All that lies on the tiny mattress is a neatly folded blanket.

The Party's Just Getting Started

IT WAS AT A FILM PRODUCER'S ROOFTOP garden party, talking with two maraschino cherries, that Adam learnt his ex-wife had moved into town. The cherries were maybe twins, he wasn't sure. Their stalks were bobbing, their lips artificially glossed and reddened. He'd met one of them before. She was a performance artist. 'I heard Guggenheim,' she was saying.

'Nothing's been decided,' he replied, looking about for his wife.

'Yeah, but like –' there was the faintest cruel glisten of an upcurl to her lip, 'the director loves her.'

'He's gay,' said Adam.

'Course he's gay, honey,' she returned inconsequentially.

'Blushed-salmon blini?' asked a waiter.

'Sweetie-honey, you need sunblock,' said the other cherry to Adam, ignoring the hors d'oeuvres. 'Your shoulders are burning up.'

A guy in chain mail joined them and nodded at Adam's crotch. 'Love the costume.'

Adam felt their three pairs of eyes skimming his body and wished he was wearing more than a pair of hand-painted underpants. 'Eve's idea,' he shrugged in reply.

'She's so ironic,' said one of the cherries nasally.

'What I wanna know is how she keeps that figure after five kids.'

'What *I* wanna know is how she's getting shows at the *Guggenheim* after five kids.'

Adam was used to people discussing his wife as if he weren't present.

'Hey,' said the chain-mail guy, turning to him, 'so your ex-wife's moved into my apartment block.'

Shaken from his reverie, Adam almost choked on his blushed-salmon hors d'oeuvre. 'What?' he spluttered. 'Lili? You mean Lili?'

'Did you just say ex-*wife*?' one of the cherries practically yelled. 'You have an ex-wife? How come I didn't know about this? You didn't tell me he had an ex-wife!' she exclaimed, turning to the guy in the chain mail.

'Didn't know till she moved in down the hall.'

'You cannot be serious. Don't tell me you were married before Eve.'

'We were young,' said Adam, still struggling with the salmon in his windpipe.

'But you and Eve,' the cherry persisted. 'I just don't believe this. I mean, we always thought you must have been like childhood sweethearts or something.'

He knew exactly what the woman meant, that there was no way in the world a woman like Eve could have fallen for a guy like him unless it had been way before she became famous. Right now though, all Adam could think was *Lili, fuck, Lili*.

He glanced around, trying to find Eve in the throng of cowboys and nuns and superheroes.

Eve was over by the pool, talking with the film producer and a young actor who'd won an Oscar already for some performance Adam had never seen. She stood head and shoulders above the crowd, her hair streaming over her pale freckled shoulders, smiling at something the actor had said, that smile that had once adorned a million billboards and earned her a cover shot on *Vogue* magazine, all before she'd even picked up an Olympus OM30 to take her first portrait photograph. He'd given her that camera, and now everyone who was anyone just adored her work – its honesty, its integrity, its *soul*. Eve could earn more in an afternoon than Adam used to in a year of landscape gardening. Eve, sweet-natured and intelligent in a way no woman that beautiful ever deserved to be. Eve, who did a full hour of yoga every morning before she even had breakfast, who drank only white wine and never ate red meat, who saw her acupuncturist every week, who had photographed the country's greatest living individuals and then some, and who still never forgot to leave a silver dollar under the kids' pillows when they lost a tooth. Standing by the pool in a hand-painted string bikini, Eve looked incredible.

Little wonder the cherries were bitter.

'You know what,' Adam apologised, 'I'd better go check on the kids. Will you excuse me a second?'

Adam stepped away across the crowded terrace. Past beautiful girls in glittering costumes, their backs honey-tanned and bare, past men in togas and RayBans. He grabbed for another glass of champagne as a waiter brushed past, and swallowed it in one.

So Lili was back in town.

And then all of a sudden there she was, walking down a leafy street near the park, with dark sunglasses over her eyes, a cigarette in her mouth, and a young Latino trailing from her shoulder.

Just keep on wheeling the stroller, she's not going to look your way, he told himself, at exactly the same moment as his ex-wife came to a halt on the sidewalk.

'Adam? Fuck, is that you?'

'Lili?' he said, jerking his head up with feigned surprise. His tone registered a notch too high. Nine-year-old Abe flashed a smirk at his father to demonstrate he'd noted her use of the f-word. Trust fucking Lili to swear in front of the kids. 'Lili, *wow*,' he continued, flailing. The Latino had on his face a look of contemptuous boredom. 'I don't believe this. My God, you're looking –' he scrabbled frantically to find an appropriate word, '*great*.'

Flattery could never fail to distract Lili.

She dropped her eyes in a lipstick-stained smile, and for a moment Lili almost did look pretty, pretty in the way a faded streetwalker could look for a millisecond when they first grabbed your arm in the street.

The truth was Lili looked terrible. An overstepped parody of herself, like she'd lurched out of a Nan Goldin print. Gut-wrenching. Like a Goldin transvestite, her face clogged with foundation and her flesh bulging from beneath her corseted top and tight leather pants. Her hair was a dirty bleached blonde, short and uncombed, dark at the roots. How could he *ever* have been attracted to this woman, was the thought that went through Adam's head. She was so not his sort. So sleazy. *So* unlike Eve.

And then, before he could stop himself, he remembered absolutely the feel of her thighs clamped around him. That noise she used to make with her throat as she came. *I have got to get out of here*, thought Adam, as he stood there with his hands still on the stroller handles.

'So what the fuck are you doing here, Adam?'

Adam held his grin. 'Saturday morning. Just going along to the park. Taking the kids out,' he continued, as if it needed an explanation. He gestured towards his progeny in the hope that maybe if she acknowledged them she'd tame her language. 'The kids,' he said, by way of introduction.

She gazed down at the three of them. 'Hi.'

'Hi,' Abe and Azura replied, equally unenthusiastic. Kids were like dogs. They could tell when an adult didn't like them. Seth in his stroller was chewing on a plush iguana.

'Uh, this is Francisco,' she said, running her hand down the torso of the Latino, who had turned his gaze away from the rest of them and was drawing on her cigarette. She let the s trail. *Francisssco.* He looked young enough to be her son.

'So, you're still with –'

'Eve, yeah.'

'God, that's been a *long* time.'

'Married life for you.' Adam made a frankly absurd faux-shucking noise out of the corner of his mouth.

'Uh-huh,' Lili nodded, her eyebrows smirking. 'So, Eve, yeah.' *That bitch*, said her smile.

Adam nodded.

'Dad,' Azura moaned, pulling on his arm. 'Can we go?'

Thank God for kids sometimes.

'Hey, gimme your cell number, I'll call you for lunch one day,' said Lili, searching in her pocketbook. 'Shit, where's my – ?' She continued her rummaging. 'Where the fuck did it go?'

'Sure,' Adam smiled, trying literally to push the kids out of earshot, 'let's do lunch. That'd be great.'

Lili, he thought as he walked away a minute later, *Lili, fuck.*

They met in a new fusion restaurant where she knew the head chef. Had probably *slept* with the head chef, thought Adam, when she suggested it over the phone. He'd planned to say no, of course, tell her that lunch probably wasn't a good idea, but instead he just said, 'Tuesday, yeah, Tuesday's good.'

He'd honestly meant to tell Eve, but when he came out of the shower that morning, she had already left. Not that it was a big deal, only lunch with his ex-wife. He left a note on the mirror in case Eve came back in: *Lili called. Meeting for lunch downtown. I'll collect Azura. Cain is staying late for hockey practice. A x.*

He spent almost half an hour deciding what to wear, wishing he had more than just Ralph Lauren shirts in his wardrobe. Eventually he chose a plain white T-shirt and jeans. Decided not to wear socks with his loafers.

Adam knew he'd arrive first. His ex-wife had always liked

to make an entrance. By the time she waltzed through the door, he'd read right through the menu twice and already finished a bottle of mineral water. She was as heavily made up as last time and her hair just as bed-mussed, but today she wore a floral silk dress, cut in low ruffles across her breasts, and red peep-toe sandals that buckled around her ankles, giving her feet a porcine quality.

'Am I late? Crazy morning.'

She put her cell phone and cigarettes on the table, ordered a Cosmopolitan, then gave him a flirting up-and-down appraisal. He wished he'd worn the socks.

Toying with her cigarette packet, she looked around for the waiter, 'They're gonna bitch if I smoke, aren't they?'

'It *is* illegal.'

She gave him a look.

Leaning back in her seat, Lili reviewed the other diners cursorily, then fixed her eyes back on Adam. Smiled. 'So, this is weird.'

'It's been a long time, Lili.'

'It's Lilith.'

'You're calling yourself Lilith now?'

'Lilith *is* my name,' she replied coolly. 'You looked at the menu?'

'Glanced.'

'Go for the lobster. Jean-Claude's a total genius.'

'Jean-Claude?'

She crossed her arms on the table. 'So, tell me about your exciting life.'

'That's kind of a big question to start things off.'

'Well, what do you want me to ask you about?'

'I don't know.'

'Are you happy?'

'Sure I am.'

'Well me too.' She lit a cigarette and lowered her eyelids slightly as she drew on it.

Adam looked away and threw an embarrassed smile at the

couple at the next table. 'The waiter's going to tell you to put that out, you know.'

'So I'll stub it out when he gets here. You gonna have the lobster?'

'I'm allergic to seafood, you know that.'

'What a drag,' she said, narrowing her eyes. The waiter drew up neatly alongside her elbow. 'I know, I know.' She lowered her eyelashes to the man and with a shameless pout of her lips stubbed her cigarette out on a side plate. 'I'll have the lobster. And another Cosmo.'

It was strange how you could remember so fast what you'd grown to hate about a person. Adam wondered if she was thinking the same; he noted she hadn't ordered an entrée. Lili was picking now at a lobster claw with a small silver utensil, holding the pinkie of her picking hand curled out in the air.

'So, you gave up the landscape gardening business to be, like,' she paused, 'a *house-husband*?'

'I'm happy bringing up the kids.'

'Uh-huh,' she sounded unconvinced.

'Eve loves her job, I was getting tired of mine. You know. She's having a retrospective at the Guggenheim,' he blurted.

Lili cocked her head. 'Don't you have to be dead to have a retrospective?'

'Dead,' he granted. 'Or famous.'

'Or fucking the director,' she said with a shrug.

'He's gay.'

'Of course he is. I was talking hypothetically.'

Adam clenched his napkin in his fist and felt his chin take on a defensive thrust as he looked away. 'Eve's not fucking the director.'

'Everyone knows that, sweetie. She's way too nice for that.'

'What do you know about Eve?'

'Everyone knows about Eve. Your wife's famous, honey.'

'Well, she's not fucking the director.'

'Sure she's not.' She dabbed at her lips with her napkin.

'Anyway, guy's gay as a fucking goose.'

'Exactly.'

'Exactly.' She set her napkin down on the table. 'God, I wish I could have a cigarette.'

Adam chose to say nothing. After a while she turned back to her meal. With an offhand arch to her eyebrows she said, as if it had just slipped out, 'I dream of your cock, you know.'

'*Lili!*' Adam seethed, looking around quickly to see if the people at the next table had overheard.

'Don't Lili me, honey. I'm only telling you the truth.' She shovelled a forkful of rucola leaves into her painted mouth, marking the white cotton tablecloth with dark balsamic splashes. She'd marked everything. The napkin was smudged with her lipstick, her cigarette butt was red-ringed at the tip. Her dirty stain was left on everything she touched. 'Wake up so fucking wet,' she said, her mouth still full.

'*Hell*, Lili,' he said again, and looked away angrily. Did she always have to be so crude? She was like a one-trick pony, and he'd seen this trick God knows how many times before. Boring, that's what she was. Goddamn boring.

'What about that guy you were with?'

'What guy?'

'Puerto-Rican looking.'

'Him? Francisco? He's twenty-two.'

He gave a scornful laugh. 'That's pretty young, isn't it?'

'Is it?' She looked up without a smile.

Adam had lost his appetite. His meal was only half eaten, but he dropped his napkin on the plate. Across the table, Lili held her eyes on him for a long moment, then picked up the other lobster claw and began to tease at the flesh.

For a while there was silence between them. Then, casually, she just said, 'And everything's blown over about –'

'About what?'

'You know.'

He gave her a look before he decided to reply. 'It wasn't Eve's fault.'

'Nobody says it was. I'd have done the same thing. No question. And way before she did, I tell you.'

'Well.'

'Don't give me your wells, Adam. What surprises me is you. I mean, gee honey, you were always so,' she paused, 'so fucking principled.'

'Can we stop talking about this?'

'Touché?'

'Lili.'

'Is it ever kinda weird when you're buying apples at the supermarket?'

'Drop it, Lili.'

'Okay okay, just one last question.' She held up a palm, the lobster fork still pinched between forefinger and thumb. 'Would you do it again? I mean, if you were in that situation again, would you?'

'Lili, what did I just say?'

She pursed her mouth, and stared at him sharply to register her offence, then appeared, to Adam's relief, to have decided to forget it. She laid down the claw and leant back in her seat, one hand pulling at the neckline of her dress, smiling loosely. He refused to meet her eye.

This meeting had been a huge mistake.

Adam glanced round for the waiter. 'I'd better get the check. I'll be late to pick up Azura from choir practice.'

Out of the corner of his eye, Adam saw her slip her finger beneath the silk neckline of her dress, stroking gently the top of her breast. 'I just can't get over it. This life you've made for yourself.'

'Yeah, well.'

'You're so domestic. How many is it you have?'

'How many what?' he said, knowing full well what she was referring to.

'Kids.'

'Five,' he said stonily. It sounded like a vast number as he said it, an unreasonable number, an irresponsible number, an old-joke-no-longer-funny of a number. 'Only five.'

She just nodded, trying to control her smile.

'Well,' said Lili, 'isn't that nice.'

By the time he'd put the kids to bed Adam was exhausted. He knew he should put Cain's hockey uniform in the laundry basket and hang out Abe's swimming towel to dry, but for now he just stayed where he was, lying on the couch. He was thinking about Lili, and wondering how many men she'd slept with since she'd left him. Wife excluded, Lili was the only other woman he'd known intimately in his lifetime. Where had she been all these years? What had she been doing? He realised now he hadn't even asked any questions.

'It's Lilith,' she had again corrected, the last thing she'd said before turning to the street to hail a cab.

In his breast pocket, Adam's cell sounded. It made him jump. He pulled it out clumsily and flipped it open.

Eve it said on the display.

'Hey, babe. It's me. I can't hear you. You hear me?' There was loud music in the background forcing her to yell. 'I'm at Mario's. The party's just getting started. You want to call a sitter and come down?'

Adam stayed where he was after he hung up, his cell resting on his chest.

Eve wouldn't be home till late, then. He'd have to tell her about his lunch with Lili tomorrow. He'd tell her when he brought her her morning coffee, make her laugh over the story.

Or maybe she'd be hungover. Too much white wine. She'd tell him to shut up and leave her to sleep.

She probably wouldn't be interested anyway. It wasn't such a big deal. Just lunch with his ex-wife, nothing special; he'd probably never see her again after today. What would Eve care?

Yeah, maybe he wouldn't even tell her.

Night after Night

I WAS PEELING THE POTATOES FOR OUR TEA when the sweep of bright headlights across the kitchen window caught me eye. 'Look at that, love,' I called out to him in the front room, 'Coppers in the courtyard.' And I stood up on me toes, leaning against the sink to try and get a better view.

Thinking on it now, I suppose it was a bit peculiar that he didn't say nothing back to me nor get up from his chair to have a look. Stan just turned off his radio show and finished up his cup of tea and sat there waiting, as if he knew it was our bell they was going to ring.

'Don't you worry yourself, Joycie,' he told me as he stepped down the hall to answer it, 'you go and get on with the dinner now, I'll sort it out.'

I couldn't for the life of me think why they'd be ringing on us. Took off me apron and fluffed up me hair in case the two bobbies at the door was going to want to come in, but then Stan come back with his coat and hat on and tells me he's gotta go down to the station to answer a couple of questions.

'Couple of questions?' I said. 'What do they want with you? What's going on?'

I could see them coppers out on the doorstep watching the two of us.

'And what about yer tea?' is what I wanted to know.

'Put it in the oven,' Stan said. 'I'll have it when I get back in,' and he gave me a quick peck on me forehead.

You might think that after eight years of marriage you'd know everything there is to know about your husband. Truth of it is I didn't know everything about Stan, not by a long chalk. But then look at my life and . . . well, let's just say he didn't know the half of it neither. But them were the times, weren't they? Meeting new people; you knew better than to ask questions.

Came across Stan down in a shelter, would you have it? Right during that last run of raids. Squashed up like sardines we was. He'd spent the war in London, he told me, working in a garage. Couldn't join up on account of his flat feet. Wouldn't say it were love at first sight or nothing. Well, you'll have seen the pictures – he was no Errol Flynn. And there I was in me overalls from the factory. But he seemed a decent sort, and at my age I could hardly be fussy.

We started courting and was married three months later in Bethnal Green. You didn't hang around in them days – never knew what might be round the corner.

Eight years of marriage and I never had cause for complaint. We got on all right, the two of us. He brought in his money regular and he never once hit me or nothing, never even raised his voice.

So all that night Stan didn't come in, and by morning I was worried sick, I tell you. It was awfully quiet in the flat with him not there, and I didn't know quite what I should do with meself. Normally the alarm goes and I'm up and preparing him an egg on toast for his breakfast, but I didn't have no appetite. I made the bed and straightened the sheets on his side even though they was hardly even wrinkled.

Me Mum always used to say, 'In times of trouble, make a cup

of tea.' So I set the kettle on the hob and went down the hallway to open up the front door and fetch the milk in off the
doorstep, and that's when the flashbulbs went. They was all
there already, waiting I suppose for me to come out. Their cameras were snapping away at me, and there I was, stood on the
doorstep in me curlers and dressing gown. Didn't even have me
face on. 'Mrs Turbidge,' they was calling out. 'Mrs Turbidge?
Have you anything to say about your husband's arrest?'

It was too much to take in, what with them blooming flashes half blinding me and those reporters pushing forward with
their notepads. I stepped right back again and shut the door
and stood there in the empty hallway, hearing them calling at
me from outside.

I suppose that was when I knew something was wrong. It
was an 'orrible feeling. Couldn't stop me hands from shaking.
All jittery I was.

And I didn't like the fact that if Stan had been arrested, them
out there all knew my business before I did.

So I goes down to the police station, and they sit me in a room
on me own with a cup of tea to wait for the chief officer. 'I'm
afraid your husband's in a spot of bother,' he says when he
comes in, then stops, like he don't know how to go on. 'Quite
a lot of bother actually.'

That was when they told me what Stan done.

All them . . . horrible things.

I didn't know what to say. The clock on the wall ticked over
to the next minute.

'Mrs Turbidge? Are you all right?'

I couldn't help meself; the tea I'd just drunk came right up
again. All over me frock. I was mortified.

Woman off the front desk came and helped me clean meself
up. 'It's all right, love,' she kept saying, 'it's all been a bit of a
shock for you, hasn't it? Have you got someone you could go
and stay with for a few days, till things calm down?' I told her
I didn't think I did. She gave a little sorry smile.

Before I left they asked me if I wanted to see him. I stood there for a minute. Queer to think that only a few paces away, sitting alone in a cell, was a man whose shirt collars I scrubbed.

'No,' I told them. 'No, I don't think I do.'

I didn't know what to do with meself after I walked out the nick. For a while I just stood there on the pavement, getting in everyone's way and feeling as though I couldn't even remember what number bus I needed to get meself home. It was like I'd walked out into a new world and I didn't recognise nothing in it. The motor cars seemed different. Even the sky. The paving stones I was stood on.

I suppose I just started wandering. All I knew was I didn't want to go back to the flat. Not yet. Didn't want to run into all them reporters on the doorstep, all them nosy-parker neighbours. And I didn't know what I'd do once I was back in. Knowing that he weren't coming home.

There was no one I could visit neither. Stan and me kept to ourselves mostly, and those friends we did have I couldn't imagine calling on right now. What was I supposed to say? 'You'll never guess what I just found out about Stan.'

I'd come to a stop outside the Odeon on the high street. There was a film poster for an old Mae West picture Stan and me had seen a couple of years before. *Night After Night*. It was like she was looking right at me. Eyelids smoky with eye make-up, her painted mouth not quite smiling, a stream of cigarette smoke curling up past the blonde waves of her hair. As I looked at her up there on the poster, daft beggar that I am, it seemed that she was saying to me, 'Chin up, darlin'. You'll be all right. We're in the same boat, you and me. Fell in love with the wrong sort.'

I'd never been to the pictures on me own. It felt a bit reckless, if I'm honest. I bought a box of peppermint creams from the sweets girl and sat waiting for the lights to drop.

It was a comfort to be swallowed up in all that darkness. To feel that for a little while at least I could put the real world on hold. I watched all them lovely looking men and women up on the screen. I remembered Stan explaining to me once that the pictures was all just an illusion; it was nothing but light playing against a sheet of canvas. But that afternoon I believed in it all. I lost meself.

And I had a bit of a cry as well, if I'm honest. Couldn't help it. But the picture house was almost empty and I don't think anyone noticed.

When the picture finished and the lights came up I sat in me seat until everyone else had left. Then I folded up me handkerchief, put away the box of peppermint creams I hadn't finished, and took the side door out into the daylight.

As I was coming back into the courtyard one of the reporters called out, 'There she is, it's the wife!' They all turned their cameras towards me and the flashes started up again. Around us, at the neighbours' windows, I could see curtains twitching. It felt like all eyes were on me. Like it was me that was famous.

This time I didn't drop me head and scurry past. No. I thought of Mae. I imagined meself in a slinky silky gown, with heeled satin shoes, and diamonds dripping like bunches of grapes from me ears and looped in strings round me neck. I imagined how them precious stones would sparkle in the light of the flashbulbs. I imagined a silver fox fur stole round me shoulders, and me hair bleached blonde like honey, and me eyes smoky with eye make-up. I strode across our little courtyard, imagining a cigarette between me fingertips, smoke all hazy around me. I stepped up the stairs to our flat like a film star, giving that not-quite smile for the cameras that clicked and flashed around me.

'I'm ever so sorry,' I told the reporters, as I pushed past them to our door, 'but I don't have nothing to say.'

The front door closed behind me, and it was like the illusion just slipped off me shoulders. All the flash and sparkle faded

129

in the dark hallway. And there I was, alone. A sheet of blank canvas.

I kept indoors for a bit after that. With the front curtains drawn. And after a while them reporters outside all went away. I wasn't news no more.

Kept meself busy. Changed the sheets, and put out a fresh bar of soap, and chucked out the brown sauce he was so fond of with his dinner.

All his things I put in two large suitcases – his shaving brush, and his ironed shirts, and his folded-up pyjamas, and his car manuals, and his comb what still had a few of his hairs stuck in it. I was worried as the police might need to go through it all for evidence, so I didn't throw it out, just put the two cases up on top of the wardrobe.

I was doing all right until I found his cold plate of dinner in the oven. Don't know why that upset me so much. Daft, ain't it? The littlest things. Took the plate and tipped it into the rubbish bin, even though it was a terrible waste.

After that, I didn't know what to do with meself. I'd cleaned everything there was to clean, and put away everything what belonged to him. I pulled back the curtains to let the light in again, because you can't hide in darkness for ever, then sat down on the settee, and let the silence of the flat settle around me. It was hard not to think he wasn't going to walk in the door any minute, finished with his work and ready for his tea.

Outside, in the evening light, there was birds singing. And kiddies playing, down in the courtyard.

The Loudest Sound and Nothing

At night,
*   under the sea,*
*   a body drifts,*
*   surprised at the blackness of the water,*
*   the eyes rolled back and chalky.*
Her pale limbs are interlaced with rusted chains.
*   Hands bruised and swollen,*
as though a breath has filled them with a stench that tugs
*   tight at the skin.*
*   It is the loudest sound and nothing.*
*   Long hairs tangle;*
*   catch between the teeth.*

AURELINE WYNNE-EVANS LOST HER HUSBAND
at sea. While the sky was still awash with the night and the
rain and the wind. And Aureline, sat by the fire with the baby,
thinking of how they never could seem to fill those cracks to
block out the draughts. *Baby, are you cold? Can you feel the
draught, Baby?* Out at sea was her love, being buffeted by
waves, overalls heavy as lead, his eyes glassy, seawater coursing down his throat and into his lungs. And at just the same

133

moment, Aureline felt with a gasp her own life flood out through her toes – never could she bleach the stains from the carpet. Out slipped her life, in a rush at first, until finally gurgling to a close like dishwater through the plughole. Those last drips almost tickling even – she might have laughed had she not been so empty. In her arms, the baby stirred and shivered.

And now Aureline stirred without thinking, stirred the soup for her little boy, that boy whose eyes were wrong. Blank, white, and round like the fishes' eyes when they came out of the stove. *What can you see, my baby?* And he'd lift his face to her cheek, nose between dark strands of hair, feel the curves of her ear, and whisper his secrets, the visions, the sounds that bloomed before the eyes of a blind boy. Nothing she could ever imagine, not her. The movement of his lips made her hum like a tuning fork held against wood, and she could have cried it was so beautiful, could have smiled had she had it in her, had all the life Aureline ever known not spilled out upon the carpet.

Somebody looked at her, standing before the drowned body of her husband, her face unearthly, with its eyes so wide set, as if they'd drifted with time apart from the bridge of her nose. The cheeks and forehead were flat planes, sculpted from a pale stone it seemed, chill to the touch. It was a face distorted, made unnatural by the entanglement of her ties to the past, a fishing line caught and twisted beyond saving. Uncles who coupled with nieces, first cousins with first cousins, and still all of them couples who could hold hands on the streets without turning glances. Because why should it be wrong, when he picked her wild flowers and she kissed each finger before plaiting the dough for his bread? And somebody looked at Aureline and thought, how beautiful is that face, sculpted with a defiantly faulted chisel, unwittingly beautiful. But they failed to see that behind those wide-set eyes was simply space, two stencilled holes, that had they looked close they could have stared right through to the pale-green painted wall behind her.

Aureline stared – couldn't help it – at that face that was at once utterly familiar and quite strange. It was curious. She wondered how they'd done it, how they could have sculpted something so like him, and what could it be made of – wax or marble? And she thought, how clever they are. Even to the still eyelids, with the lines like faint scars running across each one. But he never wore his hair that way – so sleek and neat like a sea mammal. He never owned a comb. And still she stared and marvelled. At length, her eyes alighted on those nuzzled whorls that once were his ears, and she found herself compelled to hold out her fingers and run them across the damaged flesh, her fingertips aching to caress the soft lobes left lace-like by the nibbling of small fish. For it was this discrepancy from what he had been that told her it was him, and she knew now that beneath the white sheet lay limbs her touch had traced.

But somebody lifted an arm to hold back her hand, and she felt as a child, told not to touch. Not to touch that which had been as almost her own.

That night, at home in the dark, the baby asleep beside her, she would hold out her hands and sculpt the air and almost, yes almost, feel the shape of her husband. And each evening she would do the same, but with the steady passing of those hours of darkness, that volume she'd once known would slowly deflate, evaporate perhaps, until, one night, she would find herself in the dark, holding out her hands and feeling nothing but for the interlacing of her fingers. His shape had disappeared. And beside her the baby would stir and turn under the covers and she'd take him in her arms and coo in his ear, curled neat like an abalone's shell, and soothe until his breath regained its steady rhythm and she felt his limbs go limp with sleep.

But now, here she stood before the body, somebody's hand holding back her own, admonishing her instincts, and all of a sudden she felt the cold and shivered. *Come, Aureline*, said somebody quietly. And she just said, *Yes*, and then, her eyes fixed on the thin cotton sheet pulled to his chin, *But mightn't he be cold? Can't we find him a blanket?* And again, somebody said, *Come, Aureline,* and pulled gently on her arm, led her to the door. Aureline stepped softly away, still staring, before suddenly pulling away from the grip. Stepping forward again, she lifted her shawl to wrap it across his body, nestling it close against his face, and as she did so, quite consciously, she allowed her fingertips to pass momentarily across his damaged ear lobes, felt the soft chill of the flesh and indentations that had once not been there, those dents and grooves fashioned low in the sea by curious fish.

Outside, she felt her knees give, felt her legs fold beneath her, her skirts collapse against the floor, and if someone hadn't caught her under the arms she knew her head would have given against the cold stone – a relief it would be to lie there, with gravity, collapse and lie and resign herself to the cold ground and perhaps never rise again – but instead someone had caught her, lifted her to a chair. And there she sat, around her voices she wasn't listening to, thinking how strange, how cruel, that only now did she realise she'd always been alone.

For only the enormity of space now could make her feel a part of something, and even that comfort was temporary. Her with the child in hand standing on the cliff edge, his knees knocking together, her hairs teased from below her scarf by the fingers of the wind. The space comforted her, the fact that she could look to the clouds and not comprehend beyond them, that she could look to the sea and barely see a horizon. Her child squeezed at her hand to pull her away and yet she stood firm, didn't want to leave. *What do you see?* he asked her, his words tussled by the air. She didn't reply. *What do you see?* His questions distracted her, his presence needled. Cold was his nose, cold were his fingers as the wind slapped at his ears and his shoulders, threatened to deafen him, and he willed her to answer him, to say something. He pulled on her arm and took a step forward – towards a cliff edge he couldn't see. And falling, she tugged his weight backwards, tumbling them together onto the rough heather and gravel – she, awkward upon him, crushing his arm beneath his body. *Oh my baby, tell me what* you *see?* pleaded Aureline, rolling her child into her arms, stroking at his hair, pressing his small face and faulty eyes against her neck and almost losing his words. *I see the loudest sound*, he whispered, low into her collar-bone, *and nothing*. It took the colour from her face, drained all colour into the heather below them, and she knew that what he saw was all she'd ever wanted and all she'd never known, and she handled him roughly as she pulled him to his feet, and set walking fast, too fast for his short legs, like a child with a toy on a string dragging and bumping behind it.

It was her fingers he remembered later. How deft they were. The way they slid and wove between the lines of cotton, the bobbins clicking together like marbles. And he felt their movement, their speed and dexterity without needing to see with his eyes their dancing. He loved to trace the pattern of the lace, its intricacies. And yet Aureline always wore clothes with straight edges. Dressed him the same. Brushed his hair each Tuesday and Saturday, recalling his father's uncombed locks. And still nobody cared to hide how they stared. Behind the tabletop he stood conscious of the architecture, aware how the buildings surrounding them refracted the voices and muffled the sound of the sea beyond. Heard the reeling gulls above. All the while his eyes, white spheres, would jostle in their orbits, urge themselves upwards into his skull. And somebody leaning across to peer closer at a piece of lace would find their own eyes lifting into his. Mesmerised by their movement. Sitting close behind him, seeing it all, Aureline would observe and say nothing. Her little boy's eyes jiggling pale. Guaranteeing a sale. And he'd find the change and wrap the handkerchief or neck-collar in fine tissue paper and tie it with a ribbon. When he passed it across he could feel faint apprehension and pity transferred through the tissue as his customer fumbled with words to address Aureline. Her reply was always as void of colour as her boy's eyes. Eyes which she would lean across to kiss, as if to still their movement. As if to feel with her lips what they saw. But finding no answers she'd fold away the lace and the fine tissue paper and the rolls of ribbon into her basket and taking his hand they'd exchange the morning's coins for potatoes and carrots and slabs of fish wrapped in brown paper. Brown paper of which she would, with discomfiture in her voice, request an extra square or so, that her son might have something on which to scribble.

Once home, she'd lay it out on the table and find him a pencil and sit peeling the potatoes and watching him cover the surface of the paper (and occasionally, too, the table leaking beyond the paper's edges) with scribble. Scribble which seemed to her more eloquent than any words she'd ever spoken. His hand would move in arcs and dashes and tiny spirals, and as his pencil hovered over the paper his head would dart and sway as if it too were partaking in the creation. Each time she knew that what he'd delight in would be making music, for that's how his pencil moved, like a musician playing an instrument. And sometimes she would rise from the table and go to the bedroom and from a shelf lift down a hard leather-covered case.

Through the doorway, he'd hear her snapping the catches open, hear the lid creaking on its hinge. Had Aureline anything inside her she might have cried, might have wept, might have sobbed to see the polished wood of her husband's violin. The mark on the base where his chin had worn away the varnish, a pallor on the neck where sweat or the warmth of his palm had paled the wood, the foot of the bow curved smooth beneath the pressure of his fingers; these marks were too physical a trace of him. How she wished her own body had been similarly branded by his presence in life. Wished she could still see the soft pressure of his fingertips on her breasts. Wished his kisses had burnt light scars upon her flesh. She wanted to scream because her body was utterly unblemished, smooth and clear as soap. Wanted to scream because she could not weep, because once upon a time her life had trickled out upon the carpet as her love had drifted further beneath the waves, seawater coursing through his veins.

In the other room, her son had stopped his scribbling. He sat quiet, waiting for her, his nose curling at the starchy scent of potato peelings, his ears listening to her every movement. And each time, Aureline, forgetting how her little boy might have loved its music, found herself wrapping the polished instrument back in its cloth. Quickly and methodically she moved, as if the very sight repelled her. Back creaked the hinge, click click went the catches, and Aureline rose to replace the case up on the shelf before returning to her potatoes.

Once, only once, she left her child alone in her desperation to feel the enormity of space. Before departing, she stood at the foot of the bed watching him sleeping, the covers bunched close around him, the dull lamplight diffuse across his face, his eyelids rocking with the dreaming sway of the lost pupils beneath. She closed the door quietly behind her so as not to disturb him and began walking fast. Over the crest of the hill she came head-on with a dull funnel of light, sweeping slow across her eyes and out to sea. She turned out her lamp on the cliff edge, waiting in the lull for the finger of light to roll across her again. Pulling her coat close against the wind, saw how its gusting strength tore up the sea below, felt stray raindrops dashed against her face. Again the funnel of light passed slow across her, failing to make her glance to its source. Had he seen it that night? Had it caught his eye, blinking across the waves before they swallowed him under? And only to spew him out again two days later, to spit his body carelessly against the coastline in the dying rain. Aureline at home with the baby, the walls whistling with draughts. Her baby! Why, her boy! She gasped, as if she'd suddenly recalled her senses. How could she leave him asleep, alone? The house might catch fire, for hadn't she left the coals burning in the grate, a candle flickering at his bedside? Turning on her heel, Aureline began to run, believed that was smoke she could smell spiralling though her nostrils, believed she'd run over the hill crest and confront flames.

While all the while there he lay, quiet within the walls, quiet beneath the covers, and quiet below his eyelids churned his dreams undisturbed – safe as the inner core of a Russian doll. In her panic, Aureline had forgotten her lamp on the cliff edge. But what could she care for a lamp when her little boy was safe, sleeping peacefully? Watching him, she remembered how she'd loved to watch her husband sleep. Asleep like a baby. Curled beneath those same covers, his head resting heavy upon the same pillow. How beautiful he had been. His hair mussed further by sleep, his breath paced evenly. It was his eyelids she watched, his eyelids she loved, each one crossed inexplicably by a line, like a fine scar. *Was he constructed by a careful seamstress? His eyelids sewn neatly in place.* The skin was pale, purple-edged, verging on waxy; like the underbelly of a small animal. Thin shields for his dreams, betraying only faintly the rapid sway of the eyes curved beneath.

There once was a time when Aureline Wynne-Evans thought her son – blind from his birth – would know only what she told him. Until the day, lying together against the heather, she discovered he already knew more than she could ever know, she with only hollows behind her eyelids. So she combed his hair and sent him to school and by the end of the week he came home in tears and she thought, how dare they make fun, how dare they tease, they, web-footed simpletons no doubt. But she knew his eyes were only a substitute, a façade to hide the true reality of their taunts. He wasn't the only child with defective eyes, no, but the only child, yes, whose mother could sometimes barely recall her name – *It will come to me – wait – Aureline, that's what I call myself.* Only she forgot to tell them she could remember. Left her words blank and took her boy by the hand and led him from the schoolyard, feeling the harsh curiosity of young eyes upon their backs. Once he came home with a bible and she laughed, *What can they think, that you'll read it?* He said nothing. She left it in the garden, let it grow moss, realised she'd forgotten to buy potatoes that morning.

He came home one afternoon, telling a story, a silly story about a boy in his class, giggled as he told it, and Aureline Wynne-Evans looked at her son and thought, *How can I have been so blind?* She began to cry, out of nowhere, out of a vessel she'd long confirmed empty, came tears. Hers? How could they be? They fell on the tabletop, fell on a square of brown paper covered by her boy's scribbles. Each one wrinkling the brown, ruckling his pencilled lines. Her tears turned to sobs and Aureline lay her head on the table, lay her head on the eloquent scribbles and cursed her fate. Her boy had fast fallen silent, his mouth aquiver with confusion, his eyes darting anxious. He burrowed his head into her lap, his arms clutching at her middle, knees resting on the floorboards. As night fell beyond the windowsills, he remained where he was, head hidden beneath the tabletop and sheltered in her skirt.

Aureline Wynne-Evans felt his presence in her lap, felt his fingers clutching, felt her body heave with its weeping, and wished she might have loved him. And as she wished this she appeared to regain her composure somewhat, closed her hands round his head and lifted it so that she might slip from beneath him. Carefully, she lay his head on the chair seat, smoothed his hair gently, and left through the front door.

What was it?
A sad-armed boy you remember?
        Shouting to the whales and fishes as his words are caught
    in the air and stolen.
Did you hit him? Push him slightly? Taunt? Was that it?
Were you ever slightly jealous as you mocked
      and saw how his eyes were far away,
           his fingernails dirty?

And you,
you went back to your family, the gas fire,
the homework underlined neatly and tea at six o'clock,
and didn't know where he'd gone to.
Was he still shouting on the sea-shore?

A Return Ticket to Epsom

THERE WAS A SMALL MIRROR ABOVE THE bathroom sink and she was leaning over to look at herself in it, one hand catching her short hair behind her left ear. 'What do you think of me?' she called out to him through the open doorway.

'I think you're drunk.' He was lying on his back on the bed, still wearing his shoes. His eyes were closed. Beneath his V-neck sweater he wore an oxford shirt unbuttoned at the collar. Both his hair and clothes smelt strongly of cigarette smoke.

'I was hoping for something a little more –' The end of her sentence was lost as she bent over and turned on the cold tap. She rinsed her face then walked through the doorway, the water dripping to her collar. Half-way across the room she stopped. 'But hey, really, do you think I'm crazy?'

He let out a groan and rolled over so that he could lift himself on one elbow. 'Why is it that you girls who hang out in bars wearing turtle-necks, with copies of Sartre on the table . . .'

'Hesse,' she corrected.

He couldn't help himself smiling. She was standing on the carpet in the low light of the lamp wearing just a blouse and a pair of pale pink knickers. Her legs were very white. He liked that. 'So tell me why,' he continued, 'girls like you with *Hesse* on the table always think you're crazy?'

'*You,*' she said with a smile as she sat on the edge of the bed and began to unbutton her blouse. 'And why do the boys who pick us up always think they're so bloody clever?'

He curled his arm about her waist and pulled her onto the bed with him, then began to kiss her, running his hand beneath her unbuttoned blouse and down to the small of her back. She lifted her head so he could kiss along her jawbone. Her hair was cropped very close to her head like a young boy's. Her bare knees were bent together and resting on his thigh. He pulled her closer to him so her legs straightened in parallel with his own.

'I'm not going to sleep with you,' she said over his forehead.

He edged the tip of one finger between the skin of her back and the tight elastic trim of her bra. 'The ones with Hesse on the table never do,' he said. 'At least not until the second date.'

'Bastard,' she laughed, her shoulders shrugging. 'Can you even remember my name?' She had pulled away slightly and was lying with one hand resting under her head as she faced him.

'Paige.'

'Congratulations,' she said, pulling a look of mock surprise. 'Can you remember mine?'

'No,' she said inconsequentially, and then she laughed. 'Actually, I honestly can't. Isn't that funny?'

'I don't really know,' he said, looking across his shoulder.

Suppressing her smile behind tight lips, she watched him for a moment, then nudged the side of his nose with her own and he turned back to kiss her. His mouth tasted of alcohol. Her hand was resting loosely upon his own, with the arm angled behind her awkwardly. Despite himself, he was conscious of the faint pressure of her fingers, how they anchored his hand lightly at the curve of her waist. After a while he leant back against the pillow, facing her. Her lips were red from kissing. 'I'm not so drunk, you know,' she said.

'You're not so sober either.'

She shrugged, then with a smile reached one hand towards his face, and gently, with the tips of her fingers, closed his eyes.

When he woke, his mouth felt dry, and he had a slight erection pressing against his trousers. He'd been dreaming, he realised, a dream that had been forgotten on the instant of waking. He rolled into a seated position with his legs hanging over the side of the bed. He was wearing his shoes and the lamp was still on. His neck felt stiff from having lain cramped beside her on the single mattress. He massaged it now with his hand, then looked to the bedside table for a glass of water. She was still asleep behind him.

There was no water beside the bed, just an alarm clock and a small pile of books – one splayed open upon the others. He stared at the turquoise numbers on the clock face until, with a quiet click, the next minute flashed onto the display. It was 03:39. He reached for the open book. As he lifted it, a pencil that had been trapped beneath the teepee of pages rolled off the tabletop and fell soundlessly to the carpet. He didn't reach to recover it. Instead, he turned over the book in his hand and began to read from the top of the page. It was in French. She'd underlined the words she didn't know. Almost mechanically, his eye scanned slowly down for them. He'd taken advanced French in his freshman year, and knew most of the words she'd marked. Still, she hadn't spoken badly in the bar that evening when the waiter had come to take their bill. He closed the book and put it back on the pile, then yawned.

Staring ahead, it surprised him to see something familiar. His watch was sitting on the edge of the desk. A clunky, expensive-looking watch his parents had given him for his twenty-first birthday and which he wore with some embarrassment. He must have taken it off before he lay down – the catch sometimes irritated the patch of skin at the inside of his wrist. He rose from the bed, carefully so as not to wake her, and, pulling at his right trouser leg, stepped across to the desk and slipped the watch back on his wrist. On the desktop was a sheet of A4 typing paper – a computer print-out showing a grainy photograph of a racecourse, men and women wearing boaters and bustles pressed hard against the rails. One horse was about to gallop from the bottom-right corner of the frame, another rounding the turn a few metres behind. On the ground between the two lay a dark mass. It could have been a fallen horse, or a body. Underneath the image, as if a note in reminder to herself, was written, *They found a return ticket to Epsom in Davison's handbag.*

Again he glanced to the photograph, but without much interest, then secured his watch and turned back to where she lay. Her back and shoulders were covered by her blouse. The skin at the nape of her neck was prickled where her hair had been shorn close. Up-flung across the pillow, the fingers of her right hand curled in a loose fist. He could hardly see her face from where he stood, but his eye followed the curve of her hip as it smoothed into the length of her bare thigh. It was very quiet in the room.

In the stillness of that moment, what struck him suddenly was how easy it would be for him to do exactly what he wanted. He almost laughed at the simplicity of it. This girl on the bed, she didn't even know his name.

For a full minute he remained where he was, watching the girl, then abruptly he turned and moved across to the small bathroom. A light hung above the mirror. He flicked the switch and stared at his reflection, unsmiling. His eyes looked tired. After a few minutes he took a green plastic tooth mug from the shelf and emptied out her toothbrush and a tube of toothpaste, then filled the mug with water and drank. He drank three cupfuls before he placed the mug back on the shelf and wiped his mouth with the back of his hand. Turning, he lowered the toilet seat cover and sat upon it. Through the open doorway, he could see her white legs stretched out upon the bed sheets.

My Brain

DIEGO IS STANDING WITH LISETTE, AND
Lisette is not standing with his mom, who is waiting on the
other side of the Chinatown map clutching her bag as if someone might want to snatch it.

And Brian, Brian is late.

He missed his subway connection by like three seconds
because a woman from the casting department called and
wanted him to copy that script for her before she left to go
drink cocktails in some hotel bar or whatever it is women
from the casting department do when they leave work. And
the question now, wonders Brian, as he dodges the crowd
toward his mother and his girlfriend and his girlfriend's four-
year-old son, is who is he supposed to greet first?

'Mom, hey!'

'Brian,' she exhales, as if he's at least an hour late.

'Sorry, Mom, I'm sorry. Work, traffic –' She smells of clean
linen and Amarige as he kisses her. Lisette and Diego are staring at them. He wishes he didn't feel so nervous. 'So Mom,
hey, I want you to meet –'

One finger on her elbow, he directs her attention across the
cartographic Chinatown. She sees Lisette. Her smile holds, but

her eyes flash her son a look which Brian is a hundred per cent sure Lisette picks up on.

'Baby,' he says in greeting, touching Lisette's waist lightly instead of kissing her. She's wearing cut-off turquoise tights with ballet flats, a denim mini-skirt, and a red and purple striped sleeveless top with no bra to contain the girlish breasts perking beneath. Her body stiffens ungivingly against his fingers. 'You brought Diego, hey!'

'Is it a problem?'

'No. Gosh, no. Always great to see my buddy!' Brian holds up a fist for Diego to knock.

Over dinner once, Brian's mom had announced that she didn't believe in teenage pregnancy. 'Like, you don't believe it happens?' his sister Megan had snorted. 'Or just that any girl stupid enough to fall pregnant before she's married and financially tied to a man is hardly deserving of your sympathy?' Their father sent Megan up to her room. Spending mealtimes in her room was a phase she had to grow out of. Megan was in her final year at SUNY Albany now and marrying a med student in the fall.

'My cousin didn't show, what was I supposed to do?'

'No problem,' Brian grins. He swallows an inbreath. 'No prob-le-mo.' He ruffles Diego's curls and notes that the kid is dressed almost identically to himself – cropped Tommy Hilfiger pants, Nikes, white undershirt, chunky-link silver chain around his neck. When did four-year-olds start dressing like grown-ups? Brian nods his head and smiles at them all. 'Great to see you, Mom,' he says, brushing a finger against her shirtsleeve. 'So, we hungry?'

He wants to take them to this Sichuanese restaurant the production crew took him to a couple of weeks back. It's the kind of place you'd only find if someone took you there, with incredible food and terrible service and hand-written misspelt signs on the walls detailing the specials. Brian loved it. Across the table could be a famous actor, or a Pulitzer prize-winner, or a road sweeper – it was that kind of place.

'I really think you're going to dig it,' he enthuses. 'It's an experience. The food's totally authentic.' His mother nods, and turns a horrified glance to a row of mahogany-shiny roast ducks strung up in a restaurant window. Lisette cuffs Diego upside the head for some misdemeanour Brian didn't catch. He slips his arm around her waist and brushes a happy kiss against her temple. She looks good. And Brian's feeling good now, walking along this busy Chinatown street with his arm round this beautiful girl, and his mom on his other side, and knowing he's got his first paycheck in his wallet and at the end of the evening can just peel off the bills and treat them.

But when they walk into the restaurant, it all looks some-how dingier than he remembered it. The linoleum floor is lit-tered with paper napkins and chopstick wrappers, the tables overcrowded, the plastic dishes sloppy with food, the strip-lighting bright. His mother smiles graciously as the Chinese waiter barks instruction for them to sit down at a table in the middle, and Lisette just wrinkles her nostrils, 'It's pretty busy in here.'

'We share tables, baby. It's a great way to meet people. It's the Chinese way. It's like Chinese tradition.'

'You mean you don't even get your own table?'

'Baby,' says Brian, kissing her on one ear lobe.

Lisette is the first girl who makes him think in poetry as she undresses for him. He loves her slender caramel-brown limbs, and her spiralling dark hair. He loves her heavy-lidded almond eyes and her wide pink lips. She's beautiful in an inescapable way, and she knows it. She's the first girl he's slept with who never finished high school and has a scar across her belly where a baby was pulled out. 'So you've got a kid,' he'd said when he asked her about it. 'That's cool.' But the truth is, despite the scar, he can't quite believe Diego came out of her. He can't believe someone just a year older than himself could have a child of their own. Lisette doesn't act like a mother. Or not his idea of a mother, anyway. And Diego's just like a kid brother who hangs around a lot. Fun to goof about with.

On the top of Lisette's arm is tattooed *Emanuel*. The Hispanic valet she met in eleventh grade who fathered Diego and wouldn't take responsibility till she had a paternity test done. 'You wanna pay, I'll take it off,' she told Brian. 'But don't think I'm getting *Brian* in its place,' she said with lifted eyebrows, letting him wrestle her back to the bed.

He sees his mother looking at the tattoo and decides to turn attention to the menu. 'So shall I order egg rolls?' he asks earnestly. 'What does everyone want? Wonton dragon soup? They've got this amazing fried seaweed in ma la sauce I want you to try. And the tea-smoked duck is incredible – we've got to get an order of that.'

'You think Diego's going to eat seaweed, Brian?' asks Lisette, her tone clipping Brian's enthusiasm. 'Tea-soaked duck?' She fixes her gaze on him, awaiting an answer.

'He doesn't like Chinese food?'

'Look, I don't want to be up all night with him.'

'Does he have a delicate stomach?' asks Brian's mother.

Lisette keeps her eyes on Brian.

When Brian returns with Diego's Happy Meal, neither his mom nor Lisette are talking. His mom is feigning interest in her wonton soup, Lisette is sitting with her arms crossed on the tablecloth, her plate of food pushed away from her, the chopsticks dropped at angles upon it. 'Diego, I've told you already. Behave,' she complains, as the boy tries to wriggle under the tabletop.

'Food's up, buddy,' says Brian, setting the Happy Meal down. He smiles a 'hi' at the Chinese family that have joined them on the other side of the round table. They ignore him. 'So how we doing?' he says eagerly, sitting back in his seat. 'Isn't it great?'

'Very fresh,' says his mom. 'Sichuanese food, is it always this spicy?'

Brian sees Lisette's discarded chopsticks. 'You already finished?' he asks with concern.

'I can't eat that,' she says, tipping Diego's fries out for him on the tabletop.

'It's too hot for you?'

'Yeah, it's too hot,' she says. 'And there's fucking seafood in it. You know I don't eat seafood.'

Brian holds a finger up to his mouth, hushing her. 'Language, baby,' he whispers, glancing up to see if his mother has noticed. 'Look, I didn't order anything with seafood, I know you don't like seafood.'

She stares at him, her perfect eyebrows raised. 'I heard the waiter say oyster sauce,' she says, laying stress on each word.

'There are no oysters in oyster sauce, baby, everyone knows that.' He gives her thigh an affectionate squeeze under the table but she jerks her leg away.

'What's that then?' With one of the chopsticks, Lisette points at her plate.

'That's a Chinese mushroom.' Brian tries to laugh but she won't even smile at him.

'Yeah, whatever.' She squirts out some ketchup on the tablecloth beside Diego's fries. 'You want the dipping sauce for your nuggets, baby?'

Brian watches her, unspeaking, forgetting his mother for a moment. 'They'd have given us a plate for that, you know. You only had to ask.'

'It's a paper tablecloth, Brian, they're gonna throw it away.'

Brian's family have a small townhouse in Brooklyn. They bought it before Brian was born, before real estate agents started knocking on the doors all down their street asking if people wanted to sell. 'Well, if you change your mind,' they used to tell Brian's mom. 'This could be a very attractive property for an investor looking for somewhere to fix up.' 'But we live here,' she'd tell them with something like affront. 'This is our home.' She'd drop their business cards in the wastebasket.

But their words made her look around the rooms with uncertainty – did the walls really look like they needed repainting? Were the kitchen units looking tired?

Brian's father has to travel a lot for work. He missed a lot of birthdays when Brian was a child. When Brian was ten, his mother hired a portrait painter advertising in the art school where she took her pottery class. The family portrait he painted still hangs in the lounge. Megan's hair is side-combed. Brian is wearing a button-down shirt. Their mother has on the heirloom pearl necklace that she keeps hidden at the back of the boiler cupboard in case they're burgled. The painter had to do their father from photographs because he missed so many sittings.

Brian's mother had Megan straight out of college and never took a job. It wasn't an issue for her, she was never career-driven. She enjoyed motherhood. Her husband's frequent absences never much worried her. It's not that she isn't close to him, but there was something special about the triad she and the two young children formed when she was on her own with them.

She entertains herself with hobbies now – swimming, needlework, reading – and would describe herself as more than content, if you asked. She holds subscriptions to *Newsweek* and *Life* magazine and once started to write a self-help manual but it didn't get far. She's thinking about joining a book group. Since Megan announced her engagement, she's found herself lingering before shop windows hung with baby outfits, but something like superstition holds her back from purchasing clothes for a grandchild not yet conceived. Women have children later now, she tells herself, they want careers. Brian's mother makes sure to speak to her children at least once a week now that they've left home. It's important to her to stay close. Late at night, as she lies in bed in the dark, she longs sometimes for the time when they were young, quietly asleep in the bedrooms next door. What she would give to just once more enter the night-light glow of their childhood rooms, standing there knowing these small sleep-breathing pyjammaed children needed her.

'Tell me about your job,' she says to Brian, distracting him from the ketchup on the tabletop with a finger brushed against his arm. 'Is it still going well?'

Most days Brian loves his job. He loves the passion his colleagues share for each project, how everything is go go go, the magic of standing on a dark film set watching the actors. Occasionally it gets him down when somebody ordering him to fetch a new film reel, or photocopy a pile of documents, or carry a table back to the props cupboard can't even remember his name. They're busy people, he tells himself, it's understandable. There's no better job to be in if he wants to make this his career. 'The opportunities, Mom. I'm getting to know all the right people. It's like, all the time you're learning. I got to fetch lattes for Michael Douglas the other day.'

His mother smiles.

'It's just crazy, being able to hang out with people like that. I tell you, the job is exhilarating. The people are – It's like this exciting life you want to be a part of, you know.'

'I heard from Trudi Berryman that Christopher is transferring to Cornell. You heard from him lately?'

Brian's smile deflates. He shakes his head. 'I've got a job now, Mom. I'm not going back to college.'

'I respect that, but . . . You used to love school so much. "Brain", Daddy and I used to call you. You remember?'

'Until I started pulling bad grades.'

'That's not true.'

Lisette shifts in her seat, watching Brian's mom impassively.

'You haven't called me Brain for years, Mom.'

His mom looks down to the unfinished plates of food and doesn't know what to say.

'I'll get the check,' says Brian flatly.

'You know what I found?' his mom says, without looking up. 'The other day, behind the kitchen radiator? You remember that card you made me after the school trip you took to the Museum of Natural History? You remember? "When I grow up", you'd written,' she starts to smile, '"I want to be a dinosaur."' His mom laughs. 'You remember that at all, Brian? "I want to be a dinosaur."'

'I think you should leave Brian to live his life as he wants,' says Lisette.

Brian's mom stops. She looks to the young girl dating her son, then across to Diego, sticky with ketchup and barbecue dipping sauce. 'How old is he?' she asks quietly.

'Four and a quarter.'

'Make the most of it,' Brian's mom says. 'They grow up so fast.'

Brian hails a cab for Lisette and Diego. 'We can take the subway,' she complains, 'we don't need a cab,' but he pushes the money into her hand and she lets him kiss her before she climbs inside. 'Get in here, Diego,' are her parting words, 'I wanna get back.'

When they've pulled off, he hails another cab for his mom. 'I'll take you home,' he tells her.

'You don't need to do that, Brian. I'll be fine. You can't come all the way to Brooklyn.'

But he climbs in anyway and she doesn't protest further. Neither of them says anything as the cab takes them through evening streets down across the city. Brian watches the people on the sidewalks and up at lit windows in the apartment buildings they pass. He doesn't feel like going back to his apartment with its broken boiler and his roommate Tyler who'll be smoking a joint in front of some trash TV. He could go back over to Lisette's, but the bell will probably wake Diego and then she'll be pissed at him. What he wants, he realises, is his old bedroom, with the blue night-light and the glow-in-the-dark stars on the ceiling, but it no longer exists, not anywhere – last winter his parents stripped the astronaut wallpaper and turned his room into a study.

They pull up outside the house he lived in for most of his life this far, and Brian insists on paying the driver, feeling how much lighter his wallet is from when he started the evening.

'I'll get the subway back,' he tells his mom.

She's waiting on the sidewalk for him. 'I think Daddy's home.' She lifts her head to the lights behind the front curtains. 'You want to come in and say hi?'

Brian looks up at the windows for a moment.

'It's okay. You're tired. I'll give Daddy your love.'

Her son nods. He wraps an arm around her shoulder to hug her, and as he pulls back again, 'Mom –' he wants to say, but at that same moment she cups his cheek in her hand.

'My Brain,' says his mom.

On Pale Green Walls

I REMEMBER THE FIRST TIME I SAW HER. IT
was almost Christmas. It hadn't snowed yet, I don't think, but
the night was ever so sharp and felt like needles when it hit
your face. On the way, we pretended to be smoking, clamping
imaginary cigarettes between our lips before exhaling with a
billowy mist of breath.

I didn't even notice her at first, there was too much to look
at. Everyone was moving and stamping warmth back into
their feet, their silhouettes lit by the shivering light of the candles. They were brushing past us, three times larger than usual
for the layers of clothing they were wearing, and it all smelt
different – exciting and special. With a tweak to the pompom
on my hat, an old man wrapped in great swathes of furry pink
mohair halted for a moment and looked into my face. He
stood only a little taller than I, back curled like the paper end
of a party-hooter. Frightened by his wrinkles, I shrank into my
mother's legs.

With a yellow-nailed hand, the old man grasped for my arm
and pushed a plastic-wrapped boiled sweet between my fingers. A second later he was swept along by the crowd and I
was left holding his sugary offering. It was purple, the sweet –

blackcurrant flavoured probably, my favourite – but I could still feel the dryness of the old man's touch, imagined flakes of his skin clinging to the sticky surface of the sweet, so I let it drop to the stone floor. Within a moment, a heavy booted foot had stepped on it, and there it lay, shattered in its plastic wrapper.

I must have been wearing at least five or six layers that evening, several jumpers, woolly tights pulled above my belly button, a thermal vest tucked into my knickers. All she had on was a blue dress, blue like water in a swimming pool, and a funny white shawl over her head. She stood higher than the rest of us, surrounded by candles.

My brother had to keep prodding me so I'd turn back to my hymnbook. Hers was the prettiest face I'd ever seen, all pointed down except for the eyes which arched upwards. I thought she was an angel; didn't know any better.

By the time we came to leave, I was so tired that my father had to lift me into his arms. As we walked out I looked back at her over his shoulder. She was still standing there, unmoving, in that dress the colour of swimming pools.

You know how it is when you learn a new word and then you begin to hear it all the time? It was like that with her. I started to see her everywhere we went. Coughing and spluttering with post-Christmas flu, my mother took me to the doctor's surgery and there she was in the waiting room. Then I saw her in a bookshop, and at my brother's school, and even at my grandmother's house. She'd let her hair down at my grandmother's. It reached to her waist in long dark waves. For weeks after, each time I looked in the mirror, I'd tug furiously at my short pigtails and I cried when my mother took me to the hairdresser's to give me a neat bob.

One Sunday, I was lying on my stomach on the living room floor, drawing a picture of a ballet dancer pirouetting on an elephant's back. My father was sitting in his chair, hidden behind his paper. There was a great noisy shuffle each time he turned a page. After a while I looked up, and there she was, on the front of his newspaper, a huge black and white photograph of her. I guessed she must have been quite famous. But something was different. In her arms she held a baby. I stared at that baby's face and hated it as I'd never hated anything before. She was looking down at it, smiling at its bald head, and I could tell how she loved it.

The telephone rang and my father lay down his paper and left the room. I stretched out my arm, pulled the front page towards me. Glaring down at that shiny baby face, I knew instantly what to do. With my pencil I stabbed two holes where the calm tiny eyes were and then, taking a red crayon, I drew blood coming out of its mouth and a dagger in its heart. Contented, I pushed the paper back and returned my attentions to the pirouetting ballerina. My father came in again, smiled at me, and I smiled at him. He sat down, picked up his newspaper, and then I heard him draw in a breath very sharply. Looking up, I saw his face, still with horror, his eyes fixed on the blood and gore in front of him. He turned to me, then back to the massacred baby, then back to me. I remember thinking that if he stared any harder his eyes would pop out from their sockets, imagined them rolling off his lap and across the carpet.

'Did you do this?' he asked me. His voice was very serious. I nodded, but all of a sudden I was scared. He seemed terribly angry.

'Why on earth, Violet? What could have compelled you?'

I shrugged. He called out to my mother. First hesitantly, and then again with more force. She came in from the garden, her face expectant, still wearing her gardening gloves. My father held the bloody baby out to her and she gasped, her gloved hands coming up to shield her face. I hid my head in my arms, the carpet tickling at my nose. I pressed my shoulders up against my ears to muffle their voices, but I could tell my mother was upset. She swooped down to me. 'Why did you do it, Violet?' she asked, pulling my head from my arms.

I knew then that you must never draw on newspapers.

The next day, having left my brother at football practice, we went back to the church. All the way there I zigzagged along the pavements, trying not to step on the cracks, but my mother was irritable and kept grabbing my sleeve and pulling me along so that I couldn't help but let my feet fall on the gashes between paving stones. I looked back for the bears but we were walking so fast I suppose they didn't have time to come out. Just outside the post office, my mother met a friend of hers and the two of them launched into conversation. I was holding her hand, and after a while I began to lean out from her and swing.

'Violet!' she scowled.

We were standing underneath a tall tree and I began to kick at the dust at my feet. Cradled in a pocket of earth was a tiny bird. Barely a bird, in fact – the creature had been halted at a state before birdhood – more a curled-up embryo, surrounded by the wreckage of its fall, the slivers of pale blue eggshell. I pulled at my mother's arm to reach closer to it. It was about the size of a fifty-pence piece, purplish in colour, too young to have feathers. Its teeny beak had been nudged into its chest, its legs twisted, and the eyes were slammed shut. I stared at it in fascination and wonder. My fingers itched. I stretched out, and over, and grabbed at it just before my mother tugged me back to her side with an irritated, 'Violet!' She didn't see me slip the tiny creature into one of the mittens dangling on a string from my coat's arm.

A wide old man in a black dress welcomed us in. It was a dark day outside and the church seemed dull and cold. There was none of the warmth and bustle of that Christmas night. I pushed forward to peer around the old man's skirt, wanting to see if she was still there. To my delight, she was. She hadn't moved at all, but the halo of candles was gone and she stood shivering in the stone arch. We took echoey steps down the centre of the church, straight past her and into a small room that led off on the left. It smelt as if there was dust in the air and damp in the walls. Great piles of hymnbooks teetered in the corners. Children's paintings were Sellotaped haphazardly above them. The old man flicked a switch so that one spring-like bar of an electric fire began to glow orange. A framed sepia print hung on the pale green wall above the fire. It was a faded photograph of a group of black tribesmen holding feathered spears and wearing minuscule loincloths. Three stiff-looking gentlemen in black dresses stood between them.

She was there, just next to the window, and that pleased me, but she was holding that horrible baby again so I glowered at its piggy face.

My mother had already sat down and begun talking to the man, but turned round at this point and pulled me towards her. From her handbag she withdrew the photograph from the newspaper, unfolded it carefully, and gave it to the old man. He reviewed it quietly, scrunching up his thick eyebrows and pursing his plump mouth. He looked at me, back at the photograph, and then back to me. Then he leant forward. The plastic chair he was sitting in squeaked as he leant over. I wanted to giggle because it sounded like he was farting, but he was moving so close I just stayed still. I'd never seen anyone with hair coming out of their nostrils before. When he spoke, his words smelt of old eggs so I tried to hold my breath.

'Why did you do this, my child?' His left hand gestured to the paper he held.

'Oh she won't be able to tell you,' said my mother. 'She's . . .' – she paused to flick her eyes over to me and then back at him – 'mute.' She always pronounced that word very precisely, pushing out her lips for the 'mu' and ending with a sharp click of her tongue at the front of her mouth.

The old man exhaled with a long 'Ooooooohhh,' and I imagined the egg smell clinging to my hair. To my relief, he sat back again with a few more squeaks of the plastic seat.

'Very worrying,' he murmured. And then again, 'Very worrying.'

My mother looked pained. She dropped my hand so that she could tangle her fingers together. 'We just don't know what to think, you see.'

Tiring of them, I turned round to stare into the glaring eyes of one of the black men in the photograph. I wondered if he had been a cannibal. Then I looked up at her, but I didn't like to see her crooning over that baby so I stuck my tongue out at it.

'Look at her!' my mother cried. 'Oh, Father! She's sticking her tongue out at the Lord!' I drew my tongue back in.

The old man's expression turned anxious. He leaned almost imperceptibly towards my mother as if she might fall at any moment and he wanted to catch her. His pink tongue licked his lips slightly and he opened his mouth to speak but then simply mumbled another, 'Very worrying'. I wondered if that was all he would say.

'Violet,' called my mother. She grabbed at my hand but missed and instead caught my swinging mitten. There was a sharp crack, like a little spine being snapped. I winced as I remembered my tiny bird. 'What do you have there, Violet?' She pulled the mitten towards her, dragging my arm with it. I think she expected to find a secret store of stolen sweets. When she saw the featherless, withered, beaky little creature she let out a scream.

The old man jerked forward to drop his hand on her knee, and as he did so the newspaper cutting fell loose and fluttered to the floor, coming to rest on the cold lino. I felt sick when I saw it. They had decapitated her. Chopped round the baby and sliced off her head. I stared at the jagged line cutting just above her pretty shoulders and it made me so angry and so sad. I darted forward to grab it and as I did so my mother snatched at my arm. It set me off balance and her tumbling after me onto the lino. The black tribesmen and stiff-looking gentlemen were knocked by my arm and fell to the floor with a smash.

Reaching for the newspaper baby, I tore him in half, crumpled him in my hands, put him in my mouth, chewed for a second, and then swallowed.

'Violet!' sobbed my mother. 'Violet!' Her voice was a thin wail. Her hand was groping at my foot. The wide old man was plastered to the far wall. His face was frightened, his mouth tunnelled into a long 'O'. He was like a photograph.

I could feel tears struggling at the corners of my eyes. I looked at the still faces of the tribesmen lying on the floor under shards of glass, then to the tiny, shrivelled chick neglected on the lino, and then I looked up to her. Even then, after all the noise and commotion, she was still calm, and perfect, and beautiful. Smiling down at that baby. That baby who I knew she loved more than me. She just stared and stared at him and didn't even turn once to glance my way. I opened my mouth to scream, and like a silent tableau we waited.

Slow Billows the Smoke

ACROSS THE LAWN, NATHANIEL IS DANCING. Alone in the morning half-light. Dressed entirely in white apart from his shoes, the leather darkening slowly as the dew seeps upwards. A veil hangs across his face so that his features are fogged, indistinct as if seen through steamed glass. He side-steps across the grass and pauses. His gestures are utterly precise, lingering. He circles ninety degrees, then takes a careful pace towards the sun bleached pale in the distance. Like a displacement of time shown on slow-reeling camera film, his movements seem in retrospect. It is as if the very air resists him. Gravity tarries his steps.

All the while they crowd the sky about him like a dense scattering of neatly sewn stitches. Poised. Watching. The silence of the morning muffles the hum of their wings.

Standing in the doorway, I dare not move a muscle for fear the sound might carry across the green and alert him to my presence. My insides echo the line of Nathaniel's movements, the data diffusing itself within my mind, lodging within the quietly compact curls of my brain. A fine hand reaches from behind and closes across my eyes.

It is over. I know it is over for I hear at least two hundred, if not more, disperse into the very vaults of heaven. His step is straight as he walks across the grass towards us. With that distant prickle of irritation he will by now have seen us through the fine mesh of his veil; a girl standing straight in a red silk dressing gown, her eyes covered by another's hand. As he passes us unspeaking and disappears within the house, the white cotton of his jacket brushes against my sleeve.

My eyes are crushed closed beneath his fingers still as Thomas leans over my shoulder and presses his mouth to mine.

* * *

His passion is apiculture.

'Apiculture? What is that word?' I kick off my shoes and stretch my legs up onto the dash. We are driving under an arch of trees and the sunlight dapples the tan of my stockings. How the bright shapes move. Fast. Like trying to watch raindrops on paving slabs. He holds the wheel with one hand, smoothes it from side to side as the road dictates, while the other hand reaches to twist the dial on the radio. 'I said, what was that word?'

He settles the needle at an early Schubert sonata. 'Apiculture. The cultivation of the Honey Bee – *Apidae* – my Céline. Say it.'

And I mouth his words carefully, watching him all the while, not trying too hard for the clipped accent because I know he likes my disregard. 'Apiculture. Cultivation of the Honey Bee, *Apidae*.' I narrow my eyes as I smile, and Thomas, giving a quick glance back over his shoulder, pulls the car into a lay-by. He leans across the leather seat and slides his hand along my thigh. The motor is still running and the Schubert plays on.

When we draw up at the house we see Nathaniel distanced by the lawn. He's dressed for the bees, but as he walks towards the car he lifts the nets covering his face and slips off his gloves. I've retouched my lipstick and am leaning forward to replace my shoes as Thomas skirts the boot of the car to open my door for me. We emerge just moments before Nathaniel reaches us, me still fiddling with the clasp on my purse. His face surprises me when I look up, so passive does it appear beneath the wide netted brim of his hat. He is marginally less pale than his outfit, with skin reminiscent of dry paper once heavily crumpled and later run through a press. He smiles only when he comes to a point on the grass just a pace or two away from us, and even then it is a slim smile, wintry.

'Hello, old chap.' Thomas has his arm about my waist but stretches out his free hand to Nathaniel's shoulder. His excitement is palpable. I feel it through the thin voile of my dress.

Nathaniel nods and holds his smile. 'Good to see you.'

'And you, you old devil.' Thomas tilts his head towards me, still grinning, his glance catching mine momentarily before angling back to his friend. 'So, Nathaniel. Meet Céline, my pretty French wife.' His laugh hangs a moment above our heads before diluting in the sky.

'*Enchanté, madame*,' says Nathaniel as he lifts my hand to his kiss, keeping his eyes in line with mine.

'*Enchantée*,' I reply, but my smile is curt.

We take the cello to the music room. This house has a hundred rooms, or so it feels. A room in which to read, to dine, to dance, to take tea, to breakfast. Rooms with closed doors that he doesn't take us into. When Thomas was a child, he used to spend his holidays here. And yet there is an awkwardness with which he follows Nathaniel's step.

Across the parquet floor, the sunlight slants its dusty path through the high windows of the music room. The walls are lined with blue brocade, the green-tinged off-white blue that surprises when you peel a quail's egg. I have to stop myself from running my hands across their silken surface. Above the mantelpiece hangs Apollo with his lyre, corpulent cherubs reclining in the foliage at his feet. Another painting is leant shyly against the wall. It is a tiny Cubist work with a guitar and a wine bottle sliced across the canvas. In the afternoon light a piano basks, its lid lifted, innards flashed; somehow indecorous as a young girl with skirts raised to sun winter-white thighs. Crouching opposite, a spindle-legged harpsichord. Above its keyboard stands a musical score, left open at a middle page as if someone had walked away mid-piece. A quartet of other instruments is positioned about the room; a viol, its wood burnished dark, a shining bugle, a filigreed harp, and an oboe resting languorous upon a wooden cabinet. They surround like an expectant audience.

Thomas takes a seat in the centre of the room and opens his cello case. He folds back the felt wrappings, careful as a mother with her babe, lets down the stand, and cradles the instrument between his legs. He tightens the bow, slides it in long slow strokes across the rosin.

'I had the room aired for you,' announces Nathaniel. He's standing against the piano, toying with a tuning fork, his right side ashen in the sunlight. He's just about to say something else as Thomas begins to sound the strings. Satisfied with the pitch, he begins with Bach. The clear notes exhale the fresh air into the room that Nathaniel's opened windows couldn't hope for. Thomas loves the precision of Bach, the understatement, and suddenly I realise that these are precisely the qualities I recognise already in Nathaniel. The thought makes me lift my eyes in his direction and I am surprised to find him staring directly towards me.

The Principle of Bee Space
Until the middle of the last century, a harvest of honey could be obtained only by killing the colony inhabiting a hive. That was until, in 1851, the apiarist Lorenzo Lorraine Langstroth discovered the principle of 'bee space', enabling him to revolutionise world practice. The distance left by bees between each wax comb is, precisely, nought point two-three of an inch. He takes a sip of tea. In light of this discovery, artificial hives could be manufactured which, allowing for this space between

adjacent combs and the end frames of the hive, prevented neighbouring combs from attaching themselves to one another. The combs could, therefore, be removed to harvest the honey and wax without the killing of the colony.

Nathaniel likes to lecture.

He places his words carefully, as though they are well-preserved specimens laid upon a display dish. These dishes he presents to Thomas. When I ask a question, it is Thomas who receives the answer.

The way in which he relates to his bees consequently surprises me. I ask if I might see them after tea, and he nods his head slightly and tells me of course I might. He disappears upstairs to retrieve some of his old equipment.

'Bees can't detect red, can they?'

'Correct, Céline,' smiles Nathaniel, glancing down the scarlet length of my dress. 'But we don't want to take unnecessary risks, do we?' And he hands us each a white suit to fit clumsily over our clothes.

Nathaniel slow-billows the smoke amongst the combs, and I can't help myself from stepping back as the bees begin to appear. Rising lazily within the smoke. With stiff-gloved fingers he lifts a sheet of comb and gestures us to look closer. It's thick with a dark mass of the insects, crawling rapid amidst the yellow. Their combined hum is insistent on the ear, rising in intensity. I reach for Thomas's hand and, feeling my touch through the cloth of his gloves, he squeezes at my fingers.

'Can you see her?' asks Nathaniel. We both lean forward to scan the densely moving creatures. My sudden in-breath tells him I have located her. Lying magnificent, not as large as I had expected, but strangely hypnotic none the less. Utterly dignified and yet also wanton, like an exquisite thing resting prone in a fur coat, long legs sprawled, wide eyes expressionless and shining. Other bees are bowed round her, their wings and antennae moving fast. 'Beautiful? Over three years old – I've never had one survive this long before.' His finger gestures towards a smaller bee circled close by an eager crowd, her abdomen waggling. 'And this one – you see her? – a worker bee. We surprised her dancing. She's mapping a path for the others. And look, look there: drones. Absolutely powerless – can't sting, can't even feed themselves. They're alive only for procreation, nothing else. And here: larvae in the cells – you see that? The workers nurse them. They'll pick out one or two of the little beggars and privilege them with a diet of royal jelly so they'll grow up to be queens.'

I turn to watch his dialogue betray the distance I've come to expect. His voice is low so as not to disturb his colony, and yet once or twice he actually stumbles in his haste to release the words from his mouth. Looking at him, I know how he longs to stroke his cheek against their velvet backs. Through the mesh of his veil I see a few beads of perspiration glint on his forehead. The hairs on his brow are terribly fine and blonde, his cheeks are flushed slightly. I turn my eyes back to the bees and feel my own cheeks redden.

'You don't like him. I can tell.'

I'm sitting in front of the mirror, my fringe pulled back from my forehead, wiping cold cream under my eyes. Beyond my face, I see Thomas pacing in the candlelight. His collar is loose, hair ruffled into dark points about his head. I look away and say nothing.

He sits heavily on the edge of the bed, his back to me, head in his hands. 'He's been like a brother to me. You could at least pretend to like him.' He exhales loudly. 'Say something, why don't you?'

I turn the lid on my jar of cold cream before looking up to his reflection. 'I think he might hear you through the walls,' I say tonelessly.

He lets his head roll back so the length of his throat forms a pale curve. 'Good God, Céline.' His eyes are in line with the cornicing.

This runs deeper than me or Nathaniel. As I stand beside him, Thomas lets his eyes drop again to mine and we both understand that. So often with Thomas, it's the notes he leaves out which hold the real passion. In their absence lies their eloquence.

I watch us in the mirror. The silken sheen of my robe glowing dully, the line of his shoulder blades, my face lost in the shadows. Slowly, Thomas runs his thin cellist's fingers down my side and, with my eyes still fixed on our image in the mirror, I am pulled to the bed. I hope he hears us through the walls.

We wake early to walk in the grounds. How lush the English countryside looks in June. Curvaceous, the hills and valleys seem about to breathe, like a parachute silk held aloft, air billowing beneath. A fine mist clings to the horizon and the soil treads damp underfoot. Cattle graze quietly in the fields behind the house. Beyond them a thick line of trees.

By the time we head back for the house the mist has risen and the day is growing warm. 'So this is where you spent the summers of your childhood?' I ask as we walk.

'This is the place.' Thomas leans his head back to take in the sky. 'Vast, isn't it? I can remember it all so well, you know. Being let out in the mornings, our hair combed in place, knees clean. And then so *tired* by the time we returned. The days just seemed so *long*.' He takes my hand, but his mind is elsewhere. 'I've never known anyone like I knew him then. We knew everything about each other. Everything.' His eyes lift. 'Speak of the devil, heh?' I look ahead, across the bowed heads of the cattle in the field, to see Nathaniel vertical before the house. A tiny figure in the distance. Staring out towards us. Standing quite still.

Thomas is playing his cello in the music room. We've left the doors open so that the sound can travel through the hallways. In the library, I'm looking amongst the shelves; many of the books relate to apiculture, others are more diverse. Often, when I slip a spine towards me, dust falls from the pages.

A noise from behind startles me and I turn around a little too fast.

179

'Oh, Nathaniel. You surprised me. I thought you were out with your bees.'

'*Not yet.*' He's speaking with my language. His accent perfect as only a foreigner can make it. He turns to the shelves on the far wall, reaches for a book with obvious indifference. He's looking down into its pages as he speaks. '*Thomas tells me you are French. That is correct?*' he asks coolly.

The question is ridiculous, made more so having been executed in my own tongue. I don't know whether to answer.

'*I'm from Normandy,*' I respond finally.

'*Ah, I know it well. I fought there.*' He continues to peruse the book before him. Shuffles the pages with delicate movements. All the while, the sound of the cello filters from the music room.

I haven't moved since Nathaniel made his presence known. He can feel my awkwardness; he's testing me. I remember something else Thomas once said, about a game they used to play. How they'd take a match and hold it under the other's hand, wait to see who'd give way first. Nathaniel could always hold out longer, whether he was holding the match or not.

He replaces the book on the shelf and continues along the wall in my direction. He's running his hand along the spines, following the titles with his eyes.

'*So you like my bees, Céline?*' His questions come offhand, or at least they sound that way. I nod in reply, and although he doesn't look up I know he's acknowledged the movement.

'*Thomas really isn't bad on his cello these days, is he?*' He's quiet, his right hand moving slightly in time to the distant music. '*He'll never be . . .*' He looks at me. '*But we both know that, don't we?*'

This time I don't nod. I don't move at all.

'*Why is it that you French women are always so beautiful, Céline?*' And as he says this he reaches forward to finger one of the buttons at my collar. I move backwards very slightly but he holds tight to the shining sphere. '*So, shall we fuck?*'

Precise, polished, the words fall like cold marbles, leaping sharply before rolling away across the wooden floor. And then I'm walking fast through the doorway, across the hall, and out over the back lawn. I head briskly towards the line of trees until I'm out of breath and only then do I look down and see the torn strand of red thread hanging where once was sewn a tiny round button.

It's growing dark by the time I walk back to the house. The lights inside have been lit and from a distance the windows are tiny squares of glowing orange cut into the blue horizon. I let myself in and go straight upstairs to our room. Thomas is sitting on the bed, dressed for dinner. He rises as I walk through the door.

'Where've you been?' He takes my hands. 'I was worried.'

'I was just walking, that's all.' I've not looked at him until this point, but now that I do I realise suddenly that there's something else hanging in the air. He couldn't possibly know what Nathaniel said in the library, he was playing his cello all the while.

'Nathaniel's bees are dead, Céline.'

'There isn't an explanation,' says Thomas in a hushed voice as we hurry down the stairs.

'But there *must* be. They can't all just have died with no reason.'

'Look, I told you before, he doesn't know what happened.' He pulls me to his side, and just before we enter the dining room whispers fast against my ear, 'Now don't mention a thing, all right?'

Nathaniel is seated at the far end of the table. Sitting straight in a high-backed chair, a glass of whisky in his hand. He barely acknowledges us as we walk in.

I see it before I sit down. There, lying centrally on the white china of my soup bowl, the button from my dress.

As I sit, I pick up the button with finger and thumb and place it next to my napkin. Nathaniel swigs back his whisky and refills his glass from a decanter on the table.

'A good walk, Céline?' As he says it, he leans across the table to fill our glasses with wine.

The evening is excruciating. The air in the room hangs pregnant above our heads; laced with the candle smoke, it's trapped against windowpanes closed fast against the night. It feels uncomfortably warm. I can feel my brow damp, my cheeks flushed. Nathaniel keeps having our glasses refilled and the alcohol presses tight below my skin. Clearly, he himself is quite drunk. Shapeless like mercury, the conversation idles awkwardly between the serving dishes and silver cutlery, pausing abruptly whenever someone enters to serve the next course.

We're sitting in silence, waiting for the port and cigars, when Nathaniel, all of a sudden, rakes back his chair and strides from the room.

I'm wondering if we should go after him when Thomas, sharing my thoughts, says he thinks it better if we leave him alone. We remain silent at the table, polite children waiting for permission to leave. And then we're jolted by a swoop of light behind the curtains and the sound of wheels turning fast against gravel.

'He's taken the car,' Thomas cries, running out through the door. I follow him without thinking, into the dark of the night. We can see the lights of the car in the distance, careening across the fields.

'The bloody fool will kill himself,' shouts Thomas. His words are almost lost, for he's running across the grass in the direction of the car. How would it look from above I wonder – the car swerving wildly as it traces its drunken path across the fields, and behind it two small figures, one several paces ahead of the other, both racing across the fields in its direction.

It works in counterbalance; when the car finally comes to a stop we move somehow even faster than we have been previously, as if its sudden stillness grants our legs new speed. It doesn't, of course, come to a halt with any practised ease – when we started to run we knew somehow that it couldn't possibly be stopped that way. It all happens so quickly, so monumentally, with a hideous, jolting crash that seems to reverberate through the very earth. And yet it's not the sound of the crash which remains in our ears as we run; instead our ears echo with an inhuman sound that rings out at the same moment – a primal, guttural bellow of pain. Thomas reaches the scene first. Dimly I see him yank at the driver's door and then another silhouette rising from the seat to be enveloped in Thomas's arms. As I draw near them, Thomas lifts his eyes to me and mouths over Nathaniel's shoulder, 'He's safe, thank God.' My breath is rasping with the force of the run, as is Thomas's. He clasps me tightly round my waist, pulling me towards them; three figures huddled together in the middle of a dark field, the sound of the night roaring about our heads.

Lying in the rough grass before the car, lit up by the beams of the headlights, is a cow. Its neck is twisted at an unnatural angle. The eyeballs are rolled within the sockets leaving pale globes threaded with red. Distended towards the light curves the huge belly of the beast, the flesh gaping either side of a sharp slice which cuts across the white hide. Already the hair is matting, turning dark as the blood flows fast. The sight is both horrifying and mesmeric. Now that we've looked, we can't turn our eyes away. And that's when we see the first of them. Crawling intoxicated from the flesh, their legs unstable, their wings sticky with blood. How slowly they emerge at this stage. Glistening against the night. And then they start to appear more rapidly, surfacing en masse from the gashed stomach of the cow. Hundreds, thousands of them. It's the noise, that rising monotone, the heady hum that assures us we're not hallucinating. They've begun to lift into the air, swarming darkly in the headlights, disappearing as they ascend into the black of the night.

I couldn't sleep. That's why I came downstairs. Followed the dawn to the open doorway. Stood there quiet in my bare feet.

Across the lawn, Nathaniel is dancing.

Norway

ON WINTER MORNINGS, THE SKY WAS STILL DARK when Enid Tythe pulled back the curtains. She liked it that way; Enid Tythe never truly felt comfortable waking to find that daylight had stolen upon her while she slept.

By the time she closed the front door behind her and set off across the field the sky had bleached just clear enough to see the way. It hung a bruised grey-blue now in the quiet half-light of dawn, a mantle of mist clinging to the edges of the horizon, the air still chill enough to cloud with her breath. In one gloved hand Enid carried a fabric holdall containing her indoor shoes, the book she was reading at that moment, her purse, keys, an apple, and her sandwiches wrapped in grease-proof paper. She walked at a good pace for a woman of her age, her stride unwavering, moving purposefully away from her solitary house, across the wide field and towards the line of trees that hemmed the distant periphery. Her own feet had beaten the path she followed; the footsteps of years of mornings before having trodden the earth so gradually and unassumingly until finally it was plain that the land itself had cleaved to accommodate her journey. Under the trees, the thicket was less submissive; she wore stout wellingtons and still the brambles tormented, plucking curses as they snagged at her woollen stockings.

A car crossed before her as Enid came out onto the road. Its driver raised his hand in greeting and she nodded in return. The houses she passed as she walked up into the village were fenced back from the street; unremarkable post-war bungalows mainly, not unlike her own. There were lights still on in several of the front windows, the rooms beyond showing indistinctly behind the net curtains.

Many of the shopfronts stood empty, the windows papered over with dusty newsprint, their painted signs peeling – butcher, greengrocer, baker. Only the neon sign of the Costcutter remained, and Green's Hardware Store, and the post office cum sweet shop cum stationer's on the corner, and then the Hare and Billet pub and an Indian takeaway that had opened a year before in the old fishmonger's premises.

The sky by now had quite cleared. There was little colour to it any more, only a chalky grey hinting at late-morning rain.

A figure was standing on the steps to the library. Enid noticed her from a distance. A young woman, it looked like, her body tensed rigid with the cold as if she'd been waiting there a while. Enid frowned, unable to make out who it could be. It didn't look like anyone from the area.

Enid disliked it when visitors arrived before opening hours. It happened rarely, but always left her feeling vaguely affronted when it did. That time was her own, the moments of quiet before the day began were hers alone to relish. Her time to set everything in order, to turn on all the lights, warm up the computer system, and select the day's books for the display shelf, the only sound the ticking of the boiler in the store-cupboard and the rush and chug of water coursing through the radiators as the heating system got itself working. When all was ready she'd prepare her second cup of tea of the day, and sit down at her desk with her book, reading until the minute hand on the wall clicked vertical and it was time to unlock the door.

'We don't open till nine,' Enid said curtly as she approached the girl on the stairs, glancing downwards to fish in her holdall for the keys.

The girl moved forward slightly but without quite transferring all her weight, as if her body were still somewhat unwilling. 'Auntie Enid?' she said tentatively.

Enid Tythe looked up, surprised, and the girl drew her lips together in a sort of tight clipped smile. Her eyes were cheerless, ringed with black liner. She was a skinny girl, younger than she'd looked from a distance. Only sixteen or so, barely that perhaps. She stood huddled in a cheap-looking coat with a fake fur collar and cuffs, her hands dug deeply into the pockets, arms pressed tight against her sides to keep herself warmer. She wore a short grey skirt and high shoes with chunky heels. Her tights were very thin, thin enough to see the goose-bumps on her skin.

She had a lean plain face, the sort of face that would grow quite forgettable as she became older, elongated like a young greyhound's, the complexion pallid. Her fine light-brown hair hung straight, a little oily close to the scalp, with a long fringe that brushed across her right eye.

'It's Tara, Auntie Enid,' she said, and forced another smile. Her lips spread wider this time revealing for a brief second a row of teeth hillocked by the metal glimmer of orthodontic braces.

Only now did Enid recognise her. Identifying in that reluctant smile the school-uniformed child from the photographs she received each year clipped inside a Christmas card; her brother's girl. 'Tara?' said Enid, her voice still edged with irritation. 'What're you doin' here?'

'Just came to say hello, didn't I?' said Tara tersely, her weight shifting backwards again with sullen rebuff. Her gaze drifted to the concrete of the library steps and she gave a blunt sniff then wiped the back of her hand quickly against her nose before digging it back into her pocket.

'No warning or nothing?' said Enid. And then, her voice

softening a little, for there was, she could see, a brittle current underlying the girl's demeanour, as if she might cry or become angry at any moment, neither of which Enid had any desire to deal with that early in the morning, 'Well, you'd better come in, then. I'll make us a cup of tea. Daresay you're half perished waiting out here on the doorstep.'

When she'd finally closed up for the day, and turned out all but the strip of lights before the door, Enid changed her shoes and buttoned up her coat, then she reached for Tara's coat still hanging in the cupboard. In the silence of the closed library, she held it up before her as if it were something very strange and a little repellent. She felt the cheap thinness of the fabric between her fingers, observed the matted synthetic tufts in the straggling fur trim. She tilted her head towards the lit glass panel in the door to the back room, listened a moment for any sound, then slipped her hand quickly inside each pocket, pulling out the contents: old bus tickets, a few coins, a promotional flyer for a nightclub, cinema stubs, strawberry lip balm. Enid slipped the things back into the pockets and draping the coat over her arm turned to fetch her niece.

The girl was lying across the seats of the two black plastic-leather easy-chairs, knees pulled up by her chest and her back curving towards Enid, the ridge of her spine pressing faintly through the ribbing of her sweater. A sliver of pale skin was visible between the sweater hem and her skirt's waistband. She'd slipped off her shoes and they stood neatly in wait now on the grey carpet beside her magazine.

Several times that day, Enid had almost reached for the telephone receiver as she wondered whether to call her brother. It was curiosity that eventually held her back; she wanted to know why Tara was there. Why she'd turned up out of the blue, forwarding no explanations when she asked offhandedly – her lack of propriety patently failing, Enid noticed, to disguise her anxiety as she awaited an answer – if she could stay with Enid for just a couple of days. If she called her brother,

Enid suspected, she might never find out why the girl had come.

'Tara,' said Enid. And then again, when there was no response. A little louder this time, 'Tara. Come on now, wake up. It's time to get home.'

The girl started, then twisted self-consciously round and slid her feet to the floor. Her left cheek was pressed pink where it had rested against the chair seat, the mark of an upholstery button denting the flesh beside her ear.

'Here, I've your coat.'

'Thanks,' muttered Tara. She stood and slipped her arms into the sleeves, then angled her feet into her shoes, losing her balance slightly as she put on the second one, her attention distracted by the darkness beyond the window. 'It's night out already,' she said, sounding surprised.

Outside, it was cold, the air damp still from the afternoon rain. Tara pulled her coat tighter around herself and stood on the library porch looking at the row of buildings across from them.

'What about school? Won't they mind if you don't turn up?' Enid asked while locking the door. She knew the row of locks from habit even though the keyholes were lost in shadow.

'Teacher-training week, isn't it?' said Tara, glad her aunt's back was turned to her. She was watching a scene framed in the bright shape of a kitchen window opposite. A woman's back, with an apron tied at her waist. She was stirring at something on the stove.

'If you say so,' said Enid.

Tara shrugged absently, watching the woman move across from the stove to the worktop then back again.

'And your parents do know you're here, don't they, Tara?'

'Yeah,' said Tara lightly. 'Course.' She bit on her lower lip, and finally lifted her eyes away from the woman in her kitchen to the blank sky above the roofline.

Enid dropped the keys in her bag and, turning, studied the

girl in profile a moment, then followed her eye-line up to the dark sky also. 'Well, you can phone them when we get back, just to let them know you're safe.'

'Thanks,' said Tara tonelessly, giving a sudden shiver as she felt the cold bite into her.

'Come on, then. Don't want you catching a chill.' Enid started down the steps. 'I take the road home in the evenings, 'cause it's too dark to see the way across the fields.'

'Is it far?'

'Half hour or so. You're not afraid of a walk, are you?'

'No,' said Tara, following after her aunt, her tone defensive.

The streetlamps ended at the edge of the village, and thereon they walked in near-darkness, the early moonlight silvery on the wet road. The surrounding landscape was almost completely flat, with only a few clusters of trees to break up the fields and one slight rise, over the top of which the road disappeared. There were few houses out here, just the odd one or two, their windows glowing yellow in the distance. Occasionally a car would pass, the headlights swaying across the two women as the wheels made a wet sound on the dark tarmac.

'You still doing well at school?' asked Enid.

'Doing GCSEs this summer.'

'Yer teachers think you'll do well, do they?'

'S'pose so,' Tara responded without much enthusiasm. 'Bs and Cs they think I'll get mostly. A for geography maybe.'

'Yer dad always did say you were bright,' said Enid, giving the girl a quick glance but without any affection.

Tara gave a shrug of her shoulders. She was looking away from her aunt across the fields, her hands still thrust deep in her pockets. The tall grass was swaying in the cold wind, and the moonlit surface of the field looked curiously like the surface of a body of water, like wavelets tossing in a squall.

'Think you'll be taking A-levels, then, will yer?'

'Probably.'

'Wanting to go up to university after, like your father?'

Tara shrugged again.

The tall grass still swayed in the wind, its surface undulating like water.

They fell back into silence, each more comfortable not having to speak with the other, until eventually they rounded a bend and Enid stopped.

'See that ditch, there?' she said, pointing to the side of the road. 'Must be two years ago now, Morgan Saunders gets a knock at his door one evening – you see his house over there? It's just dropped dark, and there's a young chap on his doorstep, a town fella. Says his car is stuck in a ditch and he needs help. Morgan asks if he wants a cup of tea 'fore they get started but the lad just wants to get on.

'Year later, Morgan saw the police notices on the Safeway message board. Turned out the fella had buried a body in the woods up there. You see the clump of trees up on the hillcrest? Buried it just before he drove his car in that ditch. Cut up in pieces it was, in two black bin liners. Only a kiddie.'

'God,' said Tara, giving her aunt an odd look.

Enid didn't notice. She was staring at the ditch, unsmiling. 'Can't help meself thinking of it each time I pass here,' she said quietly, no longer speaking to Tara.

Still watching her aunt, Tara frowned. She felt a prickling at the back of her neck. Her legs were cold. 'Did they catch him?' She was very conscious of the expanse of space surrounding them, how small they were within it.

'Aye, that they did, thank God.' Enid turned back to her niece, 'Don't you be fretting though, girl. We don't get much trouble round here.'

'No,' said Tara, as if in agreement. They started walking again, the girl glancing once back to the ditch then across again to the distant clump of trees.

In her kitchen, Enid flicked the light switch and the fluorescent strip-light at the ceiling blinked a moment then hummed bright in the dark window's reflection of a small room lined with brown melamine-fronted cabinets. Enid set the kettle on the hob.

'We'll have a cup of tea, then I'll start the supper. You can go and ring your folks, why don't you? Phone's in the hall,' said Enid, setting out two cups next to the teapot.

Beside the telephone, Tara paused. She considered whether she should shut the door, then decided to leave it open. She could hear her aunt through in the kitchen.

The phone was made of beige plastic, the old-fashioned type with a dial and her aunt's number typed on a disc of paper in the centre below the code for the emergency services printed in red. She lifted the receiver and began to dial, listening to the clicking as each number took its turn to scroll back into place.

'Mum?' she said into the receiver. 'It's me.'

She turned so her back was facing the open doorway in case her aunt should happen to look through. Spoke just a little more quietly.

'Yeah, Mum, I'm here. Yeah, she's fine. No. No, it's all right, she doesn't mind. Just a few days.'

In the kitchen, Enid stood poised with the milk jug in hand, listening.

'Yeah. Yeah, I will. I'll be fine, Mum. All right. I said *all right*, Mum. Yeah, love you, too. Love to Dad. 'Night.'

Tara waited just a moment longer, feeling the still silence of the house, then lifted the tip of her finger from where it had been holding down the cradle switch for the length of the call. The empty sound of the dial tone echoed in her ear as she set the receiver back down.

Standing in the spare room that evening after supper, Tara pressed her forehead against the cold pane of glass at the window and looked out past her own reflection, faint in the shallow light of the bedside lamp, across the dark fields to that silhouette shape of the dense clump of trees on the hillcrest that she'd seen earlier from the road.

The room was cold from disuse and the air smelt stale. She'd turned on the electric heater, twisting its dial to 'max', and the smell of burning dust now puffed out through the metal grille and began to filter through her nostrils. She found the silence of her aunt's house oppressive. It had the dead silence of a place that nobody lived in.

Turning finally, leaving an oval-shaped print on the glass where her forehead had rested, Tara pulled the curtain cord and let the drapes hide the outside world from view.

She'd hoped for the succour of television after supper to drown the quiet, but had hardly felt surprised when Enid announced that she didn't have one. Tara hadn't even seen a radio in the house. Only bookshelves lined with the tired plastic-wrapped spines of ex-library volumes, their alphabetised titles redolent with lack of appeal. Her aunt had suggested she pick one out to read, but Tara had declined, saying she had a magazine in her bag.

'That's all the young want these days, *magazines*,' Enid had said, pronouncing the word with enough antipathy to leave Tara unsure how to respond.

She had no interest now in reading her magazine, and crossed instead to the bed. There was a layer of clear plastic over the bedspread, and she pushed it to one side, letting it slither to the floor in transparent folds, and crawled, still fully dressed, between the cold bedsheets. The travel alarm clock on the bedside table showed half past seven. She sat a while, her eyes focused on nothing, then leant suddenly over the edge of the mattress and pulled her bag up onto the cover, groping within it until her fingers felt the hard shape of her mobile. She switched it on at the top corner, her fingers clumsy, and waited for the blue-lit screen to illuminate.

The indicator was blank. No reception.

'No,' Tara said hopelessly, throwing the phone down onto the patterned bedspread. She felt her throat tighten, a burning pressure rise behind her eyes. She looked about herself desperately. The room was silent. 'Mum,' she said quietly, then shut her eyes tight and pressed her fingertips hard against them.

Enid Tythe had been brought up in a household where the family bathed once a week, one after another, in a tin bath of lukewarm water. If she thought about it, she could remember the little tub, placed square on the flagstones before the kitchen hearth, the windowpanes steamed opaque; having to step from the water with a shiver to grab for the towel and then sitting before the fire in your pyjamas so as your hair might dry before bed. That was Sunday evening for you, and if you cared to make yourself absent, to go to the pictures or a dance hall, then you'd bloody well just have to wait till the next week before you could take a bath again. She retained the habit of bathing only on Sundays into later life. During the week she'd flick the switch of the two-bar heater each morning and run a sink of water for a stand-up bath while the tight coils glowed slowly into life. She had a shallow plastic bucket, a little larger than a tea tray – the same plastic bucket in which she soaked her smalls each week – which she'd stand in to catch the drips.

Enid sat now in her armchair, her book open in her lap, unsettled still since her niece's quiet request that she might run a bath, and listened to the water coursing from the tap. For the fourth time in as many minutes she read the same sentence on the page before her, still not taking in its meaning. Why, the girl was going to use all the hot water in the tank, she worried, feeling irritation at her brother for having brought up a child so wasteful. She set back to her attempt at reading, and still the water didn't stop. Surely the tub was going to run over any minute, her mind was thinking. The carpet would be ruined. Was the girl foolish or merely thoughtless? Could she have nodded off in there? Should Enid go and bang on the door?

Tara was used to having baths that allowed her to submerge herself completely in water so hot it almost hurt. She was used to pouring foambath under the tap and watching the pearlescent liquid swirling in the rush of water and the scented bubbles forming until they puffed right above the edge of the tub.

So all she thought now, when she finally turned off the tap, was how mean this bath looked without any bubbles, how less inviting the water. The pallid green of it, and there at the bottom of the tub a rust and turquoise stain trailing to the plughole where the steady drip of the tap had marked the enamel over the years. Her flesh was dull and goose-bumped from the cold of the bathroom. She dipped a toe in the water gingerly, expecting heat, but instead groaned to find the water temperature only just above tepid. She must have outrun the hot water supply without noticing. With a shiver, Tara shrugged off her towel and quickly slipped her unclothed body beneath the surface of the water.

In the living room, Enid still couldn't concentrate on the words before her. Each splash of water from behind the bathroom door, each shush of the girl's skin against the sides of the tub, impacted upon her with an almost physical jolt. So much did it bother her to have another presence in the house that in the end she simply slapped her book shut, placing it on the armrest, feeling impelled to movement, desirous of being outside suddenly.

In the cold of the night air, Enid set off across the field automatically, but then, as if on second thought, doubled back on herself so her path circled the house from a distance. She walked briskly, letting the fresh air clear her head, but her eyes kept flicking back to the bungalow. She saw the glare of the bathroom light behind the stippled glass, but no sign of her niece's subverted silhouette, which meant she must still be lying down in the tub.

Slowly, unconsciously, Enid's pace began to slacken, until she came finally to a halt. She stood alone in her wellingtons in the field of tall grass, very still, her hands in the pockets of her overcoat, just observing the house. The curtains were drawn to the spare room, so she couldn't see inside, but she was able to look right into her own bedroom, or at least see through it to the lit hallway beyond the doorframe; there was an oddness to it, a sense of detachment to watching her home from such a distance, like looking through the tiny windows of a dolls' house.

She had never stood outside her own house before while anyone was inside it and lights were on, and realised only now that it wasn't a welcoming-looking house at all. The electric light at the windows was cold. Grey almost.

Tara had come to her aunt on an impulse, out of desperation, out of a foolish belief that things would turn out differently. She certainly hadn't reckoned on her aunt's taciturnity. A girl still mired in the taciturn teenage years herself, she couldn't have imagined she'd find similar in one so old. She had expected the aunt she hardly knew to show her sympathy and concern. To tease the information gently out of Tara.

Instead it took the vomiting of her breakfast toast and marmalade for her aunt to understand.

'So that's what all this is about, then,' said Enid gravely, but with a very slight tremor to her voice it seemed. She stood with her arms crossed over her chest, looking down on her niece as she knelt on the white tiles of the library toilet's floor, her face pale as the ceramic bowl she crouched over.

Tara closed her eyes tight and dug her fingernails into her palms to stop herself from crying. There was a block of blue chemical fixed beneath the rim of the seat. The synthetic stench hurt her nostrils. She felt another wave of nausea. That unavoidable wave of nausea that had already begun to hit her each morning now.

'Oh, you silly, silly girl,' said Enid, a hint of anger in her voice. Pulling her lips tightly together she lifted her head and took in a deep breath. She looked around at the tiled walls. Below her Tara stifled a sob, the sound echoing against the porcelain.

A sigh escaped Enid's lips. 'You silly, silly girl,' she said again, her tone a little gentler this time. Bracing one arm against the wall, she lowered herself to the floor beside Tara, the two of them crushed in the small space, and reached a hand awkwardly over her niece's shoulder to pull her long hair back from her face.

'How far gone are you, Tara?'

For a moment the girl didn't answer. 'Only a month or two.'

'And the father?'

Tara gulped, then drew in a shaky breath. Her eyes were closed, mascara smudged beneath them. 'He's in Norway. He doesn't know.' Her voice was very quiet.

Enid made a tired sound. 'I s'pose your parents don't know either, do they?'

Tara shook her head, then let out a violent sob, her whole body shaking.

Enid gazed, unseeing, at the bent head of the girl beside her and thought about the library beyond the door, left untended. She wondered if anybody had come in, surprised to see the front desk empty, if they were out there now, needing her help. She felt a discomfort in her joints from kneeling down like this on the cold floor and tried to shift her position slightly. Her hand still held Tara's thin hair loosely at the nape of her neck.

The sound of the young girl's sobs reverberating in the small tiled room sounded like the keening of a tiny animal in pain.

'Come on now, girl,' said Enid softly. 'Come on now, girl.'

* * *

'You're all right, you are,' he had said when he'd finished.

'Thanks,' Tara responded wanly, but his compliment did nothing for her. She'd spent the best part of the evening buoyed on the false exuberance of alcohol, feeling cocky and flirtatious and excited by herself. Around eleven o'clock she'd teetered over the edge of being in control of her actions – it wasn't the first time she'd been this way, and the truth was that even if she could have stopped herself she didn't want to. Only now, cut off from the noise and press of warm bodies in the club, did she feel the sudden deflation of that propulsion that earlier had fuelled her. All that remained was the sweet lurch of bile-ridden Bacardi Breezer rising at the back of her throat.

She lowered herself from her perch on the toilet cistern, feeling the cold of the concrete floor press against the soles of her feet. Her tights were gathered around one knee, the empty leg trailing like a withered limb. When she went to pull them up she found they'd laddered at the thigh, so instead she simply slipped them off and bundled them in her hand, feeling the flimsy nothingness of the nylon gauze against her fingers. Reaching behind her, she lowered the plastic rim of the toilet seat so she could sit.

'Going to bloody Norway on Tuesday, else I'd take your number,' he said.

'Norway?' she said with a slight frown.

'Working in a slaughterhouse, aren't I?'

'Fuckin' hell,' Tara said, shaking her fringe from her eyes as she looked up to him, squinting against the light from the bare bulb above, 'what you doing that for?'

'Get out of this dump.' He gave a sort of laugh, but then seemed to gulp it back again almost immediately. Self-conscious suddenly in her gaze, he lifted his hands to smooth his hair back in place, then wiped them against his trouser legs, leaving a faint dull stain of hair-gel on the denim. There was graffiti on the wall behind her. He slid the fingers of his hands in each pocket and just stood there, ready to leave now. Tara felt herself gag slightly and lifted one hand to her mouth, curving her shoulders inwards. 'You all right?' he asked, glancing down.

She nodded.

'So . . .' he gave a little ducking with his chin, 'shall we go back out then, get another drink in?'

Again she nodded. 'I'll be out in a minute, okay?'

'Suit yerself.' He touched her shoulder quickly, then pulled his fingers back again. 'I'll see yer out there then, yeah?'

To open the stall door he had to turn and crush against the wall. As his legs brushed against her bare knees she felt another pitch of nausea. There was a rush of loud music and voices as he opened the main door and then the beat muffled again as it swung shut.

Tara closed her eyes, then opened them again to stop the spinning. She took in an unsteady breath, swallowing back the desire to vomit.

It was bloody cold in Norway, that was all she knew.

* * *

A book had been left open on one of the desks. A hard-backed, plastic-covered art book, the edges of each page deckle-edged from past fingers flicking through them. Enid reached for it, and as she did, paused a moment, looking at the coloured reproduction printed on the open page:

A young woman in profile, standing alone in a room reading a letter, the scene lit softly by daylight falling through a tall window. She stood before a cluttered tabletop, with a string of pearls spread across it and an open wooden box such as one might keep jewellery and mementoes in. On the whitewashed wall behind her hung a large sepia-coloured map; like a window onto distant lands, somewhere far away.

The woman wore a blue silk housecoat, tied at the front with ribbons, and an ochre dress beneath, the skirts full. Her hair was pulled back from her face, secured at the back of her head with a pink sash winding round the thickness of it. Her head was lowered as she read, and the eyes were slightly in shadow beneath her brows, the lids low. She was concentrating on the letter; not smiling, but her face didn't show sadness either. It could be a letter she'd just received, delivered to her by a servant girl, or it might have been something treasured that she took out now and again to re-read. She was in the late months of a pregnancy and the lower section of her letter, below the bottom crease, rested lightly on her distended stomach.

Such a simple scene, so human. So redolent of a life once lived, a day once experienced. There was no grandeur to it, it appeared almost uncomposed. Like a snapshot taken unobserved. One could imagine that at any moment the woman would finish the letter and fold it back again. Any moment the light might change as a cloud passed before the sun. Or she might turn, and smile or frown or give a look of surprise to realise she was observed.

'Vermeer, Miss Tythe?' asked a congenial voice.

Enid started and gave a slight gasp. Her eyes were still lost, still hanging back somewhere.

'Oh, Miss Tythe, I'm sorry,' said the voice, concerned now. 'I disturbed you.' A small hand reached to touch her lightly on the arm.

'Not at all, Mr Matthews,' she said quietly, turning to acknowledge the elderly gentleman at her elbow. She'd used his name but looked at him now as if she didn't fully recognise him.

'Are you all right, Miss Tythe?' he asked, frowning because something about her seemed strange. 'You're not unwell, are you?'

She gave a shake of her head, and as she did so her eyes appeared to swim back into focus.

He returned with a faint slow nod, his face still concerned. 'I was looking for . . .' he broke off. He was a small man, Mr Matthews, active in the committee fighting to save the library from the council's threatened closure. His hair, once very dark but now greying, still swept from a neat side-parting across his forehead. He had dark eyebrows, a straight nose, and a thin upper lip. His eyes were a light grey in colour. He was dressed in a brown tweed jacket with a white shirt buttoned to the neck and secured with a woollen tie. He had a handkerchief in his breast pocket. 'Saw you had a young girl here with you last week,' he said.

'My brother's girl,' Enid nodded.

'Oh,' he said, cocking his head like a starling, 'I didn't know you had a niece, Miss Tythe.'

'She's gone again now,' said Enid. 'Had a problem needed solving.'

'Oh, I see. And you helped her, did you?'

'Yes,' Enid said after a moment, 'I did.' She stood silent for a few seconds, then looked up to him plainly and shook her head as if to dismiss the matter. 'It's all over with now, anyway. She took the bus home yesterday morning.'

There'd been an incident a few years before with Mr Matthews. She'd caught him writing lines of poetry in the margins of the library books. Poetry of a romantic nature. Bookmarking them specifically so she would find them. She'd at first assumed that someone was having a joke at her expense until she narrowed down Mr Matthews as the culprit.

'You are responsible for this defacing of library property, are you not, Mr Matthews?' she had asked, her finger pointing sharply to a neatly scripted stanza running down the white edge of a page.

He had looked at her, and said nothing.

'Mr Matthews?' she said again, watching him.

Very slightly did his chest rise and fall with the slow movement of his breath. Rise and fall. Rise and fall. And she realised she was breathing almost in time with the man. 'Mr Matthews,' she had said, 'if you commit such an offence again, I'm afraid I will be forced to remove your borrowing privileges. Do you understand me, Mr Matthews? Please don't be writing in the library books.'

'Of course, Miss Tythe. I quite understand.' And with a slow nod, he had walked calmly away. It was the last time he had ever left a message for her in library property; she'd been glad the incident had resolved itself with so little bother.

Enid Tythe looked back down now to the printed image she'd been staring at before, and for a second again she was there, standing in the room, on bare floorboards, watching the young pregnant woman reading her letter in the soft light from the window.

'Mr Matthews,' she said, without looking up, 'can you imagine a life beyond this?'

He stood paused. Watching her. Frowning. 'I . . . I don't understand, Miss Tythe.'

And now she turned to look at him. Her eyes were very clear. He'd noticed that before, what clear eyes she had, especially for a woman of her age. The irises so pale a blue as to be almost ice-like. 'This is all I know,' she said to him.

He had no words to answer her. Instead the two of them just stood a while, between the rows of bookshelves, until Enid Tythe gave a slight smile and shook her head. She closed the book in her hands and turned to slide it into place on a shelf. 'How can I help you, Mr Matthews?' she said, her voice reassuming the brisk tone of habit. 'What is it you were looking for?'

Free

She said she didn't care where he let her off. 'Just wherever you're going,' she had told him as she climbed in, and the indifference with which she'd spoken left him uncomfortable. He turned back to the road and didn't say anything more until the truck rounded the dusty track leading up into the Andalusian village he'd lived in all his life.

'I'll leave you here,' he said where the road forked, not wanting to make it a question.

'Thanks,' she replied in that same tone of indifference, and pulling her bag across the plastic leather of the seat she turned to climb out of the truck. Just as she was closing the door behind her, he leant across the steering wheel and told her what had been on his mind: 'You shouldn't do this, you know. It's not safe for a woman on her own.' Her eyes were the colour of sand, lighter than the tan of her skin; for a second she just stared at him. 'Thanks,' she said again and closed the truck door.

He watched her in his rear-view mirror as he drove up the road, walking back the other way towards the village square. Her bag looked heavy on her shoulders. When he parked outside his house the dogs in the yard lifted their heads and looked at him disinterestedly. He could smell tomatoes cooking in the kitchen.

The sun was too hot at that hour for anybody to be sitting out in the square. All the shopfronts were closed for the siesta, the metal grilles drawn down over the windows. Only the doorway to the bar was open, a curtain of purple plush strips shielding the interior. The tinny sound of a distant radio leaked from within, its noise weak and strangely wearying on the hot air. She walked past the neglected plastic chairs and tables, past the red umbrellas advertising San Miguel beer, and pushed aside the pipe-cleaner strips of the curtain. Inside it smelt of cheap cooking oil and the cured meat of the hams hanging from the ceiling.

She thought at first that the place was empty, but from beside the ice-cream cooler in the corner a man rose and moved idly to a seat behind the counter. 'How can I help?' he said, smiling pleasantly. He looked around forty, overweight with dark hair, and had a raspberry birthmark staining one side of his face, its lace edges disappearing beneath his shirt collar. The radio was playing a song that had been a hit long before, when he was still a teenager.

'A Coke,' she said, sitting at the counter.

He turned and pulled open the door of a glass-fronted fridge. She felt the waft of cool air as the door opened then sucked closed again. He set the Coke before her.

'Glass?' he said, and she shook her head. Already condensation was forming down the sides of the cold can, like must on the skin of a grape.

He leaned slightly over to one side to scratch an itch at his ankle. 'Where're you from?'

She lifted her eyebrows as if she was thinking how to answer him. 'It's complicated,' she said, then looking over told him, 'I was born in India.'

'You don't look Indian,' pulling his hand back up from his ankle.

She shook her head. 'English parents.' She revolved the can

slowly on the countertop, leaving a damp ring of condensation.

On the wall beside the cash till a plastic fly swat was hanging on a nail. She looked at the dark crust of swatted flies caked on the white mesh. Beside it was pinned a photograph of two olive-skinned children sitting on the lap of an older woman. The photo was curling at the corners and the colours had bleached. The little girl in the photograph wore a pink T-shirt that said 'I ♥ You'. The boy's two front teeth were missing.

'They your children?' she said.

He nodded and smiled automatically as he turned to the photograph. 'Nearly grown-up now, though. He's sixteen already and she's . . . well, she's fourteen.' Smiling to himself, he leant again to scratch at his ankle. 'You have children?'

'Yes.'

He glanced back up and paused, then reached a hand to straighten a pile of paper napkins on the countertop, as if it were suddenly very important that the edges were neat. She didn't say anything. After a while she lifted the can again to her lips and drank. A fly buzzed past her bare shoulders and the song on the radio changed.

The man turned back to the photograph. 'That's my mother they're with,' he said.

She looked over again now and studied the image of the older woman in the picture. Her hair was grey and pulled back behind her neck. The wrinkles in her tanned skin looked like careful pleats in her features. She was laughing, her dark eyes tight, as if one of the children had said something funny.

'She looks kind,' she said, still staring at the woman.

'She was,' he replied. He pulled a wilted cotton handkerchief from his breast pocket and wiped it across his shining temples.

Her can was empty now. It made a dull rattling sound against the Formica as she revolved it between her fingers.

'You want another?' he said, but she didn't answer, as if she hadn't heard him.

209

He gestured his head towards the empty can, and after a minute she turned finally and stared straight at him with her strange sand-coloured eyes. 'What was the worst thing she ever did to you?' He frowned, taken off guard by the question. 'Your mother,' she continued, 'what was the worst thing?'

He shook his head to the side then looked back to her with a sort of laugh. 'That's not a thing to ask a stranger.'

She shrugged but didn't smile.

He stared at her for a moment, then sighed slightly and sat back in his seat. His hand reached to unhook the swatter from the wall, but he held it limply in his lap. Only after a few moments did he tell her, quietly without turning her way.

'Why was that the worst thing?' she said eventually.

'I don't know,' he said, shaking his head with a slight laugh. 'I don't know why I even said it. I never told anyone about that before.'

'Did she look happy?' she said quietly.

'She looked . . .' he said, then paused, 'she looked free,' and as he said it the fly that had been bothering him all morning landed on the countertop and the man, with a graceful movement, lifted the swatter and slapped it flat.

Hero I Have Lost

WITH THAT, HER LOQUACITY PETERED. IT WAS a moment or two before she continued, and even then the words seemed disembodied from the preceding conversation, as if swept loosely from a high place and uttered unconscious. 'The windows in the drawing room were open, yes, but the air was cooling. Gnats had begun to enter. I was before the mirror, already dressed for the evening, fixing my hair. Humming to the music. And Daddy, he came in and stood before the mantelpiece with his back to me, then turned and smashed the gramophone disc against the sideboard.'

They were sitting together in a high-ceilinged first-floor room, street-facing but quiet. It was late morning outside – a dull drizzle-ridden day – and though the windows were large, slatted blinds partially shielded what light there was. To compensate, a variety of small lamps were positioned low about the room. A fire burned in the grate; the temperature was comfortable. Impeccably tasteful, the furnishings were restrained and pale in hue. They indicated little about the room's owner, but then again, they'd not been chosen to reflect character, rather to put at ease any occupants who might find themselves within its walls. A large collection of books was shelved opposite the windows – they ranged widely in subject but included a preponderance of medical journals. On entering, she had whirled about and strolled behind the sofa, running her fingertips along its velveteen upholstery. She'd given a cursory glance to the rigid spines of the books before pausing to slide forth a volume – *Great Adventures on Sea and Ice*. This she had flicked through nonchalantly before replacing. She sat herself in a taupe easy chair facing the fireplace. It meant she must turn her head if she wished to look at him; he, meanwhile, faced her straight on. He noted that while she had been talking she had, without thinking, or so it seemed to him, slid off her shoes and curled her stockinged legs beneath her.

A clock above the mantelpiece ticked a rapid staccato. She turned suddenly, parting sanguine lips into a smile, 'And that, my dear, was the point at which I decided I would dedicate myself wholly to pleasure.'

'To pleasure?'

'Why yes, to pleasure. To parties and dancing and fine champagne and utter debauchery.' Her eyes reeled upwards, echoing the movement of her hands. 'Well,' she shrugged, 'it seemed as good a cause as any. And, by God, I wasn't alone. Wait, surely you were there? You can't be that much older than me and you don't look like a fighting man.'

He deferred his head a fraction and lowered his lids.

'Truly?' she inhaled brightly, her hands clapping together, 'Why, darling, you don't know what you missed! We had parties like you couldn't imagine. The children of lords and ladies daring their ankles as they executed a foxtrot. And the clubs! Holed up underground thanks to the politicians – there's still a few going, but they're not like they were. I remember a time when someone poured brandy upon the piano and set it alight. Lord, that was a night. All of us too high to take it in at first. Baby grand in flames, just like bonfire night; it was *so* exciting. Of course the smoke began to make us cough and some of the girls began screaming so we all rushed for the stairs – laughing by the time we emerged into the fresh air, laughing all the harder when we discovered it was already morning and there were workers scurrying about the streets. It was *all* so hilarious. And then the musicians started up again, right there on the street – no piano of course, the skinny little pianist was sitting in the gutter in tears – and we all carried on dancing. You really weren't there?'

She glanced to the side to catch again the slight bowing of his head. When he lowered his cranium so, the glass of his spectacles caught the light of his desk-lamp and swam green like emeralds.

'Naturally we were only mimicking the musicians, we bright young things. While the rest of town adhered to Beauty Sleep, we slipped underground and syncopated our nights, placed the emphasis on the off-beat which all the stiff-necks accented so weakly. Why sleep when you can dance? Why sleep when just a few shillings can buy you a little box of joydust?' She flicked her eyes quickly sideways, playfully, and yet in that fractional glance she had registered his reaction to her words. 'Good lord, didn't you wonder why all the girls' eyes were so bright? How else could one stride with the pace? We had smiles painted across our faces. We danced all night, coupled like there was no tomorrow.'

Her smile reclined idly as she slid her gaze back along the bookshelves. 'Oh yes, they were fine days. Heady days. To *think* of them now. All those glorious dancing girls and boys. We gave ourselves gladly. Gave ourselves madly. And then grew tired of it all!' Her laugh was bright against the pale walls. 'All those men who nibbled at my ear lobes – oh so tedious.' She turned the words towards him. The spectacle lenses drooped.

'And what was the name? Wait. That one who finally made me squirm. Who would have believed it? And such a surprise! That little chit of a thing – hiding a chest not *quite* so flat beneath the black lapels and starched white cotton. Could make me shiver with pleasure.' She could feel him watching her again. He caught her gleam, caught her run the tip of her tongue – quickly – across the rim of her upper teeth. 'Ran off to Berlin with a trumpet player – or so they said. The name escapes me. So I married on a whim, chap three years younger than myself, cheeks still soft as a girl's. Daddy a duke. I'd read about Daddy in the papers. He was a sweet young man, yes, but to be honest, I always knew he was a dead-letter boy. Didn't even cry when the day came.

'Oh please, don't look at me like that, I know I must sound quite awful but I'm just trying to be candid with you. And bloody hell, I'm sure I wasn't the first girl not to love her husband.'

He shifted himself upright in his seat. 'I do apologise, for truly I was passing no judgement. Please do excuse me if I gave that impression.'

For a moment she stared silently at him, her gaze serious, then released her face again into a wide smile. 'Forgiven,' she laughed. 'You know – don't take this the wrong way – but I can't see how all this is helping. Tell me honestly, are you reaching any conclusions yet?' She cocked her head, inviting confidentiality. 'Really, what are the odds on me walking out with a slip of paper and a diagnosis?'

'Is that what you are expecting?' He almost smiled.

Afterwards, she might have remembered him as a voluminous man, had his appearance had any effect on her. As it was, she had to grant she barely noticed others' physicalities these days. But, had she strained her wits to recall him, voluminosity might have to come to mind and – what was it? – a vaguely amphibian quality. Yes, amphibian, which was strange, because hadn't that been the only decoration within the room – a handsomely framed text-book etching of a frog?

'Well hell, *I* don't know, and it doesn't bother me in the least. But I imagine that's what Daddy is paying you for. I've met your sort before, you know, so I'll admit I had a good idea what to expect. And I'm sure you're terribly clever chaps and all but, to be perfectly frank, I can't say I believe in you.

Always asking one about dreams and what not. And I used to say, "Darling, my dreams are and will remain a secret between myself and my pillow." And anyway, does it still count if they're nightmares? Oh, and look at your little alienist eyes glinting! You're like a beady-gazed salamander. Well look, I don't feel like telling you right now. And besides, we're here to talk about what happened in Highgate.'

'And what did happen in Highgate?'

She sighed, exasperated, as if this were a question she was tired of being asked. 'You tell me. Because I'm afraid *I* don't bloody know.'

'You'd seen your father . . .'

Again, she exhaled loudly, spoke in short sentences. '*Yes*. I'd just left Daddy. Left him at a tearoom on Elm Street. That I remember. We didn't talk about anything in particular – that's what you'll be wanting to know. We talked about the weather. In fact, we always talk about the weather these days. He told me he'd heard it was going to pick up the next week – he'd had enough of the rain.' Her gaiety faltered. When she continued she did so quietly, 'But it didn't pick up, did it? Still raining now.' Alert again, 'So we talked about the weather and I poured the tea and he returned the cucumber sandwiches, complaining that the cucumber was limp. And then I left.'

'And that was it?' He smoothed the page of his jotter with the flat of his hand.

'Pretty much all I can remember.'

'Can you remember where you were going?'

'To the tube, I imagine. Can't think how I ended up in the cemetery. It's not on the route. Look, I know it's vexing, but I really don't know what happened. And it's absolutely horrible, don't you see? Nothing like that has ever happened to me before. And right now, I'd just like one of you fellows to tell me it's not going to happen again.' Her attention suddenly shifted. 'May I light a cigarette?' She was already sliding a jade cigarette case from a small beaded handbag she carried with her.

'Of course.' As he said it he rose from his desk and leant his bulk towards her. He proffered a cigarette lighter shaped like a small elephant. When he clicked his finger across its tail a flame leapt from the trunk.

'Charming,' she murmured as she bent the cigarette into the flame. She drew on it deeply and exhaled slowly through her nostrils. Neither said anything for a moment. She began to hum a tune, occasionally mouthing words but barely voicing them. Turning to him she asked, 'Are you fond of jazz?'

'Quite.' He didn't say any more.

'The stiff-necks always hated jazz, didn't they? There was something far too lascivious, too . . . too abandoned in the beat; too unbalanced, I'd say. Mother thought it wicked. To be perfectly frank, I could tell why. That music is just so bloody insidious, isn't it? You feel it, caressing your limbs like molten sugar – yes – making one jerk and sway without even thinking about it.' Again, the quick run of her tongue below her teeth. 'It was only natural they should detest it. But didn't they see, that *that* was why we loved it so? Because it stood for everything they abhorred. Because the tunes would play all night and allow one to forget.' She drew briefly on her cigarette. 'And little James, still tapping his toes to the syncopated beat, right until the very minute they shot his brains across a field in Flanders. There was one of his Negroes on the gramophone, you know, when they brought round the dead-letter. Could you grant it? Fellow's tootling on a trumpet and we learn of death. Daddy turned and smashed the disc against the sideboard.'

She was speaking ever more rapidly when he broke in, 'You've mentioned that before.'

'What?' She seemed as one deflated, all at once nonplussed. Dropped her hand to rest it on the arm of the chair, the cigarette slack between her fingers.

'Your father smashing the gramophone disc. You've mentioned it before.'

'Have I really? I don't recall. Are you sure I mentioned it?' She appeared genuinely confused.

'Yes, I'm sure. Was James your husband?'

She spoke surprised, 'James? My husband? Good God no. James was my brother.'

He held his hand above his page, the nib of his pen pointing in the direction of her kneecaps. 'Your father didn't mention a brother.'

'Didn't mention James? Are you sure?' He noted her bewilderment and nodded his head. She turned her gaze away, letting it fall aimlessly to the carpet. Eyebrows furrowed, she spoke quietly to herself before turning to him, 'Daddy didn't mention James? How very curious, not to mention James. Why ever would he not do that? I thought he was supposed to have filled you in, no?' Still her hand rested on the chair arm, the glow of the cigarette low near the butt, ash ghosting to the tip.

'He told me about your mother and your husband.'

'Well I expect he would. But not James? How odd. We all loved him so terribly much. Barely eighteen; only been gone three weeks. I can't think why Daddy didn't mention him.' He sat with his pen poised, unwilling to lower it lest the scratch of nib on paper broke her contemplation. Eventually she spoke again. 'Have you *met* my father?'

'We've spoken only on the telephone.'

'I see. He's an extraordinary man, my father. Awfully intelligent. Most awfully intelligent man I've ever met. I'm quite serious, you know. He's still extremely well regarded; they say he's brilliant, possibly the greatest logician alive. I expect you'd heard of him before, yes? The three of us – my father, James, and I – we were so very close. It was always that way, ever since we were small. Whole evenings we'd spend, just sitting on his lap, listening to his stories. A child on each knee, our heads crooked against his neck, stroking gently at his whiskers as if he were a pet of ours, an elderly Saint Bernard perhaps. I can remember it so clearly.' Her fingers lifted to her nostrils and she smiled to herself. 'That was it. Cigar smoke! His whiskers smelt of cigar smoke and the odour would cling to our fingertips. The most wonderful aroma.

'Sometimes we'd pretend to fall asleep in his arms, just so as he might carry us up the stairs to bed, looking over his shoulders at the stair carpet trailing behind us. We'd wink at one another quietly, not letting on that either was actually awake.

'Then when we were older he'd take us out walking or to a museum or a concert hall. Just Daddy and James and me.

'We were in a taxicab when James asked Daddy if he thought he should volunteer. He'd not said anything, you see. Daddy, I mean. But we'd both known that's what he'd wanted James to do, that's what he was expecting from the very moment the war began. Not that he would ever have said anything. He has always encouraged us to make our own decisions. Still, we knew it was what he wanted. You must understand, Daddy abhors cowards. What he admires is courage, the courage to stand up for what one believes in.

'As soon as James said it, he knew he'd said the right thing. He knew he had Daddy's approval. "Good man, what a fine idea, we could do with a hero in this family." That's what Daddy said to him. And I turned to James and hugged him. Heard over my shoulder what Daddy said next, "That's it, Esmé, give your brother a good, tight hug. He'll be our hero one day." And I was hugging hard but I wasn't smiling. Why? Why wasn't I smiling? You know, I hardly know myself. But it wasn't because I was scared of losing him. I was, of course, but that wasn't it. It was something deeper. It was, well, all I could think was what could *I* do? Knit socks and jerseys to post out in parcels? It's not exactly gallant, is it? Hardly takes courage. Jealousy is an ugly word – that I know well. So I sat back into the leather seat and watched them. Daddy smiling on at James and little James fairly pink with pride. London rushing past the windows. And that was when I realised that it meant something else too, something I hadn't thought of before.' A pause. 'You see, I thought then . . . I thought just then that it would mean I'd have him all to myself.'

That moment, she felt a fractional falling between her fingers and turned, just in time to see the column of cigarette ash crumble. 'Oh gracious! Look what I've done. Will it ruin your beautiful carpet?' She leant her torso over the arm of the chair to scrub with her fingers at the dusting of ash.

'Please, please don't worry in the least. It will clean.' Her movement triggered the same in him and he transferred his weight heavily. 'Please, it's nothing.'

She regained her upright posture and shifted her bent legs so that her body rested against the other arm of the chair. 'Truly, I am sorry, I'm always doing foolish things like that.' She lifted her eyebrows and smiled to him, 'Let's talk about something fun, eh?'

'Of course, we can talk about whatever takes your fancy.'

'Really? It seems a terribly strange type of treatment, this. You just leaving me to witter away. And I've got such a mouth on me. I can talk for hours, you know. I suppose it makes your life easier though, doesn't it? Imagine if I were the kind of patient who didn't say a word. Wouldn't that be awful for you? Not that you need have had any worries there. I've been telling stories ever since I could speak. We both have. We'd tell them to Daddy; entertain him for hours. How we'd all chatter. He called me eloquent.' Her eyes displayed her delight. Then she laughed and, despite the warmth of the room, something made her shiver. 'Of late, I do believe I've honed my articulacy to a horrid art. Of course *we* all chattered nineteen to the dozen. It was as though we were wound up tight each night and then, as the minutes ticked, our clockwork keys turned unbidden and we had to chatter for fear of the words just spilling from our mouths. Mind you, the irony is that nothing we said ever meant a bloody thing. All of us prattling rubbish. Not that even one of us cared. Half the time the music drowned the words anyway. And still we kept up the chattering. You know, I never felt tired in the least. Not in the least. None of us did. We all felt quite immortal, I suppose. We'd dance all night and still we didn't want to go to bed. Any distraction could tempt us.

221

'I remember coming out of Murray's into the Beak Street daylight one morning and feeling I would absolutely cry if I had to just climb in a cab and go home and then, thank heavens, Cecil de Montfort suggested – why, do you know Cecil?' She turned inquisitive towards him, 'No? Oh, he's a splendid chap! The greatest dandy you'll ever see. Remind me to introduce the two of you one day. And I remember that morning because Cecil suggested we move on to an exclusive little gathering he knew of, and I took his arm and told him to lead the way. It was just myself and Cecil and a few of the chaps from our circle. He led us down some West-End back streets and along a dirty little alley – ruined my shoes! – then in through a brick doorway and I suppose we found ourselves in a laundry, for there were sheets hung all over the place and great vats of steaming wash water and those funny little Chinamen scampering all over the place.

'I thought it a joke on Cecil's part, and was just about to exclaim so when he ducked us through another doorway. Took my eyes a while to acclimatise to the dark, there were just a few candles in the place. The walls covered by thick drapes, and the floor a rolling mass of enormous cushions. All of it in a haze, because of the smoke, so thick and pungent one felt one could lick it from the air. A couple of chaps and a girl or two lolling upon the cushions – well-groomed looking fellows in evening dress, you know the sort – all seeming quite asleep.

'And there in the centre of the room, a pair of Orientals, straight out of a child's picture book – tiny fellows in those embroidered dressing-gown oojahmaflips – one holding what looked like a knitting needle into a lamp, something bubbling on the end of it, the other dragging on a great long pipe. "Heavens," I whispered to Cecil, "What on earth are they cooking up?" And he smiled at me, flaring his fine nostrils in that way he has. "Darling, I think you know, or at the very least I do believe you could make a wild guess. Would you care to indulge?" And so I asked him, very quietly, "Would I?" His

222

reply slipped out like cigarette smoke, all in one breath, "Oh I think you would, my little one."

'Gracious, tell me honestly, am I talking *too* much? Haven't you questions you want to ask?'

'Please, you mustn't worry yourself at all. Talk all you want. It's what you're here for. But if I may beg one question, might you have been under the influence of any narcotic when the events in Highgate occurred?'

She rose from her chair and stood across from him on the carpet. She hadn't thought to replace her shoes. As she spoke she shook her head slowly. 'Oh look, you're quite off course now. It was four in the afternoon, for God's sake. I'd been having tea with my *father*.'

For a minute or so she just stared at him, disregarding his discomfort. Finally she turned away. She spoke next with her back to him.

'Look, I'm a fully fledged socialite. People read about my antics in the papers over breakfast. They raise their noses higher but, secretly, half of them wish they were in my shoes. And I'm happy to elaborate, I'm happy to recount. Why? Simply to entertain? Oh yes, I know quite perfectly the tales which will titillate, and I'm a fine performer, but that's not it. I'm keen to cosset the myth, darling. I want you to *believe* in me.' Her hand raised to finger the wooden detailing on the mantelpiece. She laughed, almost a little nervously. 'See, I know it may be difficult, I acknowledge that. Trust me; I'm perfectly conscious of the contradictions. But if you please, I urge *you* to close your eyes to them.' He watched her neat shoulders pinch as she inhaled a breath.

After a few moments she turned and spoke apologetically, 'I could do with another cigarette. Would you mind? I absolutely promise I won't miss the ashtray this time.' Following his nod, she crossed the room and snapped open the jade case, leant forward again to light her cigarette from the flaming elephant. She swept the ashtray into her left hand and then, releasing a plume of smoke from her nostrils, returned to her position by the window.

'Are you sure you want to continue?' he asked her, glancing to the clock, noting how short the minute hand still was of the hour.

'Quite,' she nodded through the thin haze of smoke.

He prodded a finger forth to straighten the silver elephant standing on the desk before him. 'Tell me, how did your parents react to your brother's death?'

'My parents?' She released a long sigh which trailed upwards with a smoky path. 'Did Daddy not tell you what happened to Mother? Oh, it was all terribly silly really. And sad, because I do think she believed in it and it quite overtook her mind. I don't know how to say it without sounding harsh – we loved her, all of us – but before James's death, mother was wallpaper. Chameleon wallpaper – you wouldn't notice her, she just blended in wherever she was. She was lovely but there was never a thought in her head. She did what Daddy asked.' Carefully, she tipped her cigarette against the ashtray. 'Then James passed away and she became quite obsessed with all that mumbo-jumbo gypsy nonsense – séances and the like. It was all perfectly ludicrous.

'Granted, it wasn't just her. She'd meet up with her ladies or have them over and then they'd hoick some poor gypsy woman off the street and set up in the parlour with the curtains drawn tight – all round the table wailing and thinking they could hear the voices of those poor dead boys. Supernatural stuff and nonsense but she believed it all until the end. She died two years later from cancer of the throat. It was pretty ghastly all in all.'

'And your father?' He was tapping his pen quietly against the desk, didn't realise he was doing it.

Her answer was delayed. She drew on her cigarette, and was finally economic in her reply, 'I didn't see much of Daddy for a while afterwards. I suppose he spent a lot of time in his study.' She turned her eyes towards the window, watched the rain though the blinds. After a minute or two she spoke quietly, 'If

I'm frank, I will admit that my life of late has been overhung by grey skies. I should have moved to Biarritz, or Rio, or the Canary Isles. Damn London. I should have moved to a place where the sun shines every day, where one spends the afternoons taking drinks under parasols, and the birds are paint-box-bright.' She quashed her cigarette in the ashtray and turned to place it on the mantelpiece. Lifted a finger to trace across the glass clock face the path of the second hand, a parting of dust trailing its wake.

When she continued, her back was still to him. 'I know what you must be thinking, that all this was but a reaction. Perhaps you're right, for it was less than a week, yes, and I was out again – little James can have been barely cold – and there I was, tight before the evening had even begun, descending into the Golden Cave off Regent Street, and pausing to lift a gloved arm and giggle as I caressed the hard thigh of the calf. In light of the situation, you must think such decadence quite immoral. Oh such gay de-ca-dence,' she sung the syllables, letting them trip slowly like a fall in a melody. Laughed slightly. 'I almost missed the irony. One forgets the word implies a state of decay. But hell, the truth of it is, there wasn't a single one of us who didn't know it was false . . . it was just, well, we were all so talented at shamming.

'To think of it now, little James barely cold. Mother out of her mind. And Father. Locked in his study! I hardly even saw him for those first two months. And then when he finally emerged . . . is it a wonder I went out dancing? To think of it now. I tell you, I laughed, I was laughing as I came down those stairs. Laughing. I announced that I wanted to kiss a darkie! The younger ones screamed, so I ran onto the stage and slammed my lips against the Negro double-bass player. Remember the whites of his eyes wide open with surprise and afterwards how bashfully he turned his head back to his instrument. Hadn't expected that. Close up, he was little more than a boy.

'And then the night turned quite sour. So long ago and yet I

225

remember it so clearly. Returning to the table and finding the men heatedly discussing the monstrosities, the limbs, the mud, the dead – little more than children. Hell, *I* understood. I just didn't *want* to relate. I wanted to dance. "But darlings, stop this dreadful banter," that's what I cried, and felt my voice – a little too high. And one of the fellows turned so sharply, and beyond the wire rims of his spectacles, I saw his eyes were cold as he told me, "It's not *all* hedonism out there." And I, feeling my skin turgid with gin, forced a smile and said, "Oh no, I refuse, I simply refuse to believe it. There can *be* only hedonism." His eyes were so, so bitter, and his words sharp – like bayonets. "Good God, don't be so facile," that's all he said, and then he turned away and downed the rest of his drink in one go. All fell quite silent then. Perfectly, perfectly silent until someone hissed across to him, "You bastard, she lost her little brother last week." Everyone's face was frozen, I remember that, as all around the music ran and jumped, and suddenly the place felt hellish, everyone writhing as though they were diseased.

'I don't know why I'm being so egotistic. We were all in it together. Everyone lost a hero, didn't they?' She laughed a little sadly, 'It's funny, because it sounds as though we just misplaced him, doesn't it? To say he's lost. As if perhaps we simply forgot him on a garden bench, or in the cupboard under the stairs, or left him in a taxicab, and may still find him one day. That's what it's like, as if he's been misplaced and we are simply left alone to keep on searching.'

He watched her shoulders, their movement reflecting the quiet rhythm of her breathing. Her silence made him awkward. 'He . . . he'll always be a hero, your brother. Even if he may be lost.'

She turned slowly, and for several seconds just looked at him, her face still. 'I wasn't talking about my brother.'

Before leaving, she asked if she might use the lavatory. He directed her to a doorway just up the stairs. She told him, 'Don't mind about me, I can let myself out the front door when I'm finished. Thank you, once again.' He requited her goodbye and returned to the study.

Having entered the room he had indicated, she closed the door behind her and turned the key in the lock. For a second she stood as though she didn't know what to do, then stepped forward, pulled the wooden cover down on the toilet bowl and sat upon it. She wrapped one arm around her middle and raised the other, her fingers fidgeting absently with her bottom lip. Her eyes were fixed in space. Occasionally an expression would flit unconscious across her face, her eyebrows wrinkle. Minutes passed this way until a play of light through the trees at the window snapped her attention back. Taking a breath she stood up. As she gave the mirror a cursory glance, her hands straightened the crêpe de Chine of her skirt. Re-emerging onto the landing, she descended quietly, retrieving her hat, coat and umbrella from the stand before letting herself out the front door.

Acknowledgements

During the creation of this book, a number of people have earned special thanks. These include:

Lee Brackstone, my editor, to whom I owe so much, not only for his unstinting faith in my work, but also for his preternatural patience in awaiting it; Florent Courtois, my good friend, who allowed me to steal his name for one of my characters; Richard Francis, my university tutor, who was there right at the beginning, and his daughter Helen, who later helped with shaping the book; Troy Giunipero, who accompanies me in life and never complains when I crawl into bed in the small hours after writing all night; Giles Gordon, my first incredible agent, who is very much missed; Praveen Herat, a fellow wordsmith and constant friend, who has always let me know he believes in me; Trevor Horwood, my careful copy-editor, who introduced me to oojahmaflips; Andrew Motion, for his encouragement; James Patchett, both a good friend and a loyal and attentive reader; Cathryn Summerhayes, who is the most ebullient and supportive literary agent I could ever ask for; my friend Wendy, with whom the woman in *Free* shares her origins; Doris Wigfall, my grandmother, who has always had faith in my writing, even when it enters territory alien to her generation; Tristan Wigfall, my brother, whose handing over of a story to Lee started the ball rolling; and of course Tod Wodicka, who read every word in here before anyone else, and has so many times steered me in the right direction when I've wandered.